INTO THIN AIR

READ ALL THE MYSTERIES IN THE
HARDY BOYS ADVENTURES:

#1 *SECRET OF THE RED ARROW*
#2 *MYSTERY OF THE PHANTOM HEIST*
#3 *THE VANISHING GAME*
#4 *INTO THIN AIR*

COMING SOON:

#5 *PERIL AT GRANITE PEAK*

#4 *INTO THIN AIR*

FRANKLIN W. DIXON

ALADDIN New York London Toronto Sydney New Delhi

ALADDIN
An imprint of Simon & Schuster Children's Publishing Division
1230 Avenue of the Americas, New York, NY 10020
First Aladdin paperback edition October 2103

Cover designed by Karin Paprocki

Also available in an Aladdin hardcover edition.
For information about special discounts for bulk purchases, please contact Simon & Schuster
Special Sales at 1-866-506-1949 or business@simonandschuster.com.
The Simon & Schuster Speakers Bureau can bring authors to your live event.
For more information or to book an event contact the Simon & Schuster Speakers Bureau
at 1-866-248-3049 or visit our website at www.simonspeakers.com.
The text of this book was set in Adobe Caslon Pro.
Manufactured in the United States of America 0913 OFF
2 4 6 8 10 9 7 5 3 1
Library of Congress Control Number 2013940526
ISBN 978-1-4424-7345-4 (hc)
ISBN 978-1-4424-5983-0 (pbk)
ISBN 978-1-4424-5984-7 (eBook)

CONTENTS

MISSING 1

FRANK

"TELL ME AGAIN WHAT YOU HEARD," Officer Lasko said to me, crouching over his spiral notebook like it held the secrets of the universe.

I sighed. "I didn't hear anything," I said honestly, for about the tenth time. I squirmed in the hard plastic chair, wondering whether my brother and I would ever be allowed to leave. The Bayport PD had taken over the Funspot amusement park's administrative offices, which I don't think were comfortable under the best of circumstances. And these were not the best of circumstances. These were pretty much the worst of circumstances.

Daisy Rodriguez, the park owner's daughter and my brother Joe's recent lady friend, was missing.

It wasn't a normal disappearance. No missed curfews, no sneaking out after a fight with her parents. No, Daisy had gone missing off her father's most prized (and infamous) ride, the G-Force—sometimes called "the Death Ride."

Let me explain.

A couple of weeks ago Funspot reopened for the season under new ownership. Hector Rodriguez had bought the park, which had been a Bayport institution for a long time but had become pretty run-down in recent years, and wanted to totally revitalize it. Step one was hiring the Piperato Brothers, famous amusement ride designers, to create an all-new amusement ride exclusively for Funspot.

That ride was the G-Force. I first rode it on opening night with my brother, his date, Daisy, and her best friend, Penelope Chung. It was, in a word, awesome. Even now that I'd ridden it countless times, I still found it hard to describe exactly what the G-Force did. It was sleek and enclosed, like a spaceship, and it's safe to say that the seats moved around in a circle, and also up and down. Images were projected in the ride's center, and loud rock music played. But the combined effect was pretty exhilarating. Riding the G-Force made me feel like I'd climbed six mountains, skied down a black diamond slope, slain a dragon, breathed fire, and also saved humanity from certain destruction.

Like I said: awesome.

What wasn't awesome was the huge hoax the Piperato Brothers had pulled to gain publicity for the ride. That first night, a young girl disappeared while riding the G-Force, right under the nose of her watchful older sister. Her restraints had been cut, and the girl, Kelly, was gone without a trace. The ride was immediately closed down, but it reopened after inspectors found nothing wrong with it. And weirdly, kids flocked to the ride like rats to the Pied Piper.

They were encouraged by a "viral video" that the Piperato Brothers put together. It showed the ride in the creepiest light possible, asking viewers if they were "brave enough to ride the Death Ride." My classmates—along with nearly all the teenagers in a fifty-mile radius—wanted to prove that they were brave enough. The lines for the G-Force swelled, even as the police struggled to find any trace of the missing girl.

Not long after, a boy—an ex-boyfriend of Daisy's, in fact—disappeared in the same way. Parents panicked. The media pounced.

We thought we'd stopped the madness when we spotted one of the missing kids on a main street and chased him to a motel, where he'd been placed with the missing girl. These kids told an incredible story: that they'd been offered a thousand dollars to play "missing" for a couple of weeks, all to pull off a hoax and get tons of publicity for the new G-Force ride.

The hoax had been arranged by the Piperato Brothers, now in jail. The G-Force was scheduled to be torn down starting tomorrow. But since the ride had been declared safe by the inspectors, Hector had agreed to reopen it tonight for one last hurrah.

And on the first ride, Daisy had gone missing.

Unlike the others, she didn't appear to have spent any time in the tiny crawlspace in the heart of the ride, built to be a temporary hiding place as part of the Piperatos' plan. In fact, she'd left no trace whatsoever.

Hector was beside himself. Joe was freaking out.

And here I was, watching Officer Lasko chicken-scratch my answer into his notebook for the tenth time.

"Can I ask you something?" I asked.

"No," replied Officer Lasko without looking up. Aha. So this was a "bad cop" night. Chief Olaf didn't seem entirely sure how to handle my brother and me—he couldn't seem to decide whether we were friends or foes. Usually he leaned toward foes.

"Do you have any clues?" I asked. Lasko looked up from his notebook and sighed. "Did she leave anything behind? Are you thinking the Piperato Brothers are behind this, or someone new?"

Just then the door to the small office we were borrowing opened, and in walked Chief Olaf, followed by Joe, who he'd been questioning. The chief's expression was pretty grim, as was Joe's. I had the feeling that Joe's answers had been about as helpful as mine.

"I think we can let these boys go home," Olaf said, nodding at Officer Lasko "Unless you have anything new?"

Lasko shrugged and shook his head. "Not really. They didn't hear anything; the music was too loud. They didn't see anything; the ride was too dark."

Chief Olaf nodded, his lips pulled into a tight line. "All right then."

I stood up, looking at my brother. His face was pale, and he looked exhausted. I knew he had to be suffering right now. Even though he and Daisy had recently broken up—he'd decided the case was more important than getting the girl—I knew he really cared about her.

"Chief?" I asked, trying to sound as respectful as possible. "Can you tell us anything? You know we were close to Daisy. We, um—we're really worried about her."

Chief Olaf paused and looked me in the eye. I could tell that he knew there was much more I wasn't saying. He was well aware of the fact that Joe and I had helped the Bayport PD solve some pretty tricky cases in the past. He also knew that we'd gotten in trouble for our amateur sleuthing one too many times. So we'd worked out an agreement with the chief and our dad: If we followed some rules and checked in with the adults while doing our detective work, we could continue to investigate.

I think that while Chief Olaf sometimes sees us as wannabe private eyes, he knows that we're kind of good at investigating. We kind of catch a lot of criminals. And I think the chief understands, on some level, that sleuthing is in our blood.

Still watching me, he cleared his throat. "Okay," he said quietly. "I'm sure you realize that this information is for your ears only, and not to be shared with anyone. I'm telling you this because I know you were close to the victim. Understand?"

I nodded, and Joe did too. "We understand," he said, an edge of desperation in his voice.

Chief Olaf continued. "We're working on the theory that this is a copycat crime."

Joe raised an eyebrow. "Meaning?" he asked.

"Meaning that the Piperato Brothers aren't behind this," the chief clarified. "They carried out the first two disappearances and the hoax, yes. But this appears to be more serious. The kidnapper is hitting closer to home, the park owner's own daughter. We think that someone saw the Death Ride hoax in the news and was inspired to try his or her own hand."

I nodded, thinking that over, and struggling not to ask the obvious question: Why? That was the first, and hardest, question in any investigation. Figure out why the criminal did it, and you often find the criminal.

Why would anyone want to hurt Daisy? To send Hector a message? To get revenge on her or her family?

Why?

Joe wobbled on his feet, and Chief Olaf caught him roughly under the shoulder. "Sit down, son." He gestured for me to get up, and pulled my chair over for my brother to sit in. Joe followed orders, still looking exhausted and stressed.

"You boys had better get home," the chief said again. "Get some sleep. Are you okay to drive?" He looked at me.

"Sure," I said. I felt weary, but not sleepy.

He nodded. "Get going, then. We'll call you if we learn anything."

I stepped over to Joe and touched his shoulder. "You ready?"

Joe nodded. "I'm okay," he said quietly. "Fresh air will help, I think."

Chief Olaf opened the door, and we stepped out into the hallway. We could hear shouting coming from Hector's office, one room down.

Hector's office was on our way out. At the doorway, I peered in. An elegant, middle-aged lady was shouting at Hector, who sat slumped at his desk.

"You let this happen!" she cried, her voice rough with emotion. "With this terrible park! You forced that poor man to sell it to us, and it's brought nothing but misery ever since!"

At our footsteps, Hector looked up at the door. His eyes contained a deep well of sadness, more intense than I'd ever seen from him.

"Frank and Joe," he said. "Are you two okay?"

I nodded. "We're just heading home, sir. The police are done with us."

Hector nodded. He looked down, then gestured toward the woman. "Boys, this is my wife, Lucy. I don't think you've met."

Lucy, Daisy's mom, looked over at us. She looked a little embarrassed to be caught yelling at Hector. "Hello," she said.

"Frank and Joe were a huge help in finding the truth about the Piperatos," Hector said.

I nodded. "I hope we can help find Daisy, too, sir."

Hector winced and closed his eyes. My skin prickled with the feeling I'd said the wrong thing.

Finally he nodded and opened his eyes. "Get some sleep, boys."

We nodded our good-byes and walked out into the dark, silent night. Funspot had been closed for hours. Everybody had been kicked out when Daisy was discovered missing. The park always felt a little creepy when it was deserted. Most of the rides had completely powered down, but a few were still blinking their bright, aggressively happy lights into the darkness.

I closed my eyes and rubbed them. I could really use some sleep.

"Did Lasko say anything interesting?" Joe asked as we walked toward the park exit.

"Not really," I replied. "Just asked me the same questions over and over. What do you think about what the chief said?"

"About telling us if they learned anything?" Joe scoffed. "I'll believe it when I see it."

"No, about this being a copycat crime." We rounded a fence that led to the exit and were plunged into near-total darkness. A few lights shone in the parking lot, but they were still too far away to do much good. We'd left the lights of the administration building behind. I shivered, and I wasn't sure whether it was because of the sudden breeze.

Joe shrugged. "It makes about as much sense as any of this," he said. "This doesn't look like the hoaxes. They didn't find any evidence that Daisy was in the little room under the ride, for example."

"Right," I said, pausing to make sure we were going in the right direction. We had to go down "Main Street"—a now-dark and deserted stretch of souvenir shops and food stands—to get to the parking lot. I nodded at Joe and led the way.

"I just don't know what the motivation is," I added. "Who would want to hurt Daisy?"

Joe nodded. "I know. Who hates Funspot that much?"

I turned around, my mouth already open to reply, but the sound died in my throat, replaced by a scream.

A dark shadow shot from behind one of the souvenir stands—arms outstretched and headed for my brother!

REVENGE 2

JOE

I SAW THE FEAR ON MY BROTHER'S FACE BEFORE the hands reached out and grabbed me. But it was still a shock to be dragged to the ground, my head banging on the hard pavement. My ears rang. I struggled to reach around and grab my attacker, but a pair of strong arms held me down.

I looked up, and out of the darkness, my assailant's face appeared.

"Luke!" I cried.

Luke Costigan had never been my biggest fan, and I had never been his. He was Daisy's ex-boyfriend—the guy she'd been planning to switch schools for, before Funspot and her mom's layoff changed their family finances for the worse.

He'd been with us when we'd ridden the G-Force together earlier that night.

He was also kind of a hostile little snot. Not that I'm judging.

Now he sneered at me.

"You did this!" he growled.

"Did this?" I asked, not following. "I did this what?"

"To Daisy!" he went on.

I looked at Frank, standing above him, but my brother just shrugged.

Luke pulled back his arm like he was about to punch me. I scrambled into explanation mode.

"Listen, man, I don't know what you're talking about! I didn't take Daisy. I don't know who did!"

Luke leaned in closer. "But she wouldn't have been taken at all if you hadn't given them the idea!"

Now I was really confused. "What?"

Frank crouched down and gently touched Luke on the shoulder. Luke sputtered, surprised, and spun around.

"Hey, hey, hey," Frank said, holding up his hands in a classic "c'mon, don't hit me" pose. "Why don't you let Joe get up, Luke? We can talk about this like men."

Luke squinted at him, then looked down at me.

"All right," he said in a reluctant voice, but he did loosen his grip on me so I could get up.

"Now," Frank said, when we were all vertical again.

"How do you think we're responsible for what happened to Daisy?"

Luke glanced down at the ground, then glared up at us. "By getting the Piperatos on the news and everything, you gave whoever kidnapped Daisy the idea."

I raised my eyebrows. "What? So you would rather we didn't catch the Piperatos?" I asked.

"That doesn't make any sense," Frank chimed in. "If we hadn't caught them, kids would still be disappearing."

Luke gave us a frustrated look. "They are still disappearing," he pointed out. "And the difference is, the Piperatos were just playing around, trying to get a story started. When I 'disappeared' off the G-Force, nothing really happened to me. I'm safe. Can you say the same for Daisy?"

I stared at him, stunned.

"That's not fair," Frank said.

Luke shrugged. "I'm sure Daisy's really glad you guys helped her," he muttered. "Helped her all the way to wherever she is now."

I felt a chill go up my spine.

Frank looked at me expectantly, like he was waiting for me to say something. But I couldn't push any words out.

Frank turned back to Luke. "Listen, man—"

But Luke was already on his feet. He brushed himself off. "Forget it," he said, frowning. "There's nothing you can do about it now. I'm going home."

He ambled off toward the exit, totally calm, like he

hadn't just tackled me to the ground. Frank looked at me and sighed.

"Let's go," he said simply, and I nodded. We headed for the parking lot.

We were both quiet for a while. Maybe a minute, maybe more. Finally Frank looked at me, concerned, and said, "You can't blame yourself."

I didn't reply at first. We walked across the dark lot toward our car. "But I do," I said finally.

Frank sighed and rubbed his eyes. "It's so late, Joe," he said, and I could hear the strain in his voice. It had been a long night after a tough couple of weeks. "Let's get some sleep and talk about it in the morning."

We managed to find our car, and Frank drove us home. We'd called Dad to let him know about what had happened at Funspot, but now, since it was so late, the house was dark. The only exception was the kitchen, which was bright with warm yellow light. On the table were two plates, covered over with aluminum foil. A Post-it Note was stuck to one.

Short-rib pot pie with potato crust, it read. *Heat up in the oven. The microwave will make it soggy. Love, Aunt Trudy.*

Frank picked one plate up eagerly. "Man, she's awesome," he mused, taking his plate right over to the oven. "What did we eat before Aunt Trudy moved in?"

"I don't know," I replied. It was hard to imagine life without our green-thumbed, foodie aunt. But my appetite had disappeared the minute Luke mentioned Daisy, and where she might be. "I'm going upstairs."

Frank already had his plate in the oven and was fiddling with the dials. He looked at me incredulously. "You have to eat."

I shook my head. "Don't feel good. I need to lie down." I headed out of the kitchen toward the stairs.

Frank trailed me. "Joe, are you okay?"

I shrugged. "I need to rest. I'll see you in the morning."

Frank looked concerned. Finally he patted my shoulder. "All right, bro. You know where to find me."

I did. And I was glad I wasn't going through this alone.

When I got to my room, I collapsed on my bed. I was so tired I felt like I was sinking for about an hour. But much as I tried to relax, sleep wouldn't come. I kept thinking of Daisy. Her smile. Her laugh. The way she would toss off a joke, a mischievous gleam in her eyes.

Maybe we weren't meant to be boyfriend and girlfriend. But I liked her. I hated to think that I had caused her harm—however inadvertently.

I tried to think of everything she'd ever told me about Funspot, everything she'd ever told me about her dad . . . anything she'd ever told me that might point in the direction of the person who took her.

Before long, pale light was shining through my window. Time to get ready for school.

• • •

"You look terrible," Frank told me when I stepped into the kitchen. He didn't look too hot himself, so if he was telling me I looked bad, I knew I really looked bad.

I leaned close enough to the microwave to catch my reflection in the glossy black surface. Yikes! Pale skin, dark circles around my red-rimmed eyes, three new zits circling my chin. I was sure to be really popular at school today.

Aunt Trudy breezed into the kitchen and smiled at me. "Morning, Joe." Her smile faded quickly. "Oh dear. Did you get any sleep last night?"

"Not much," I admitted.

She nodded, all business. "Let me get you some coffee. I made it extra strong today, for you boys."

I smiled and squeezed her shoulder. Thank goodness for Aunt Trudy. She gestured for me to take a seat at the table beside Frank, then flicked on the TV that hung under our cabinets as she hurried to the coffeemaker.

The morning news was on. *"Coming up next,"* a deep voice intoned. *"In the wake of yet another mysterious disappearance, is the troubled amusement park Funspot changing hands again? One possible buyer might look familiar."*

I gave Frank a quizzical look as Aunt Trudy pushed a hot mug into my hands. "Hector's selling the park?"

Frank shrugged. "This is the first I've heard of it. But it doesn't surprise me."

I took a long sip of the coffee. The news was coming back from commercials.

"And now, after his own daughter's disappearance, is Hector Rodriguez ready to sell the troubled amusement park Funspot—to its former owner?"

The picture cut from a smiling anchorwoman to a grizzly-looking white-haired man, who stood outside a slightly dingy yellow clapboard house. The text at the bottom of the screen identified him as DOUG SPENCER—FORMER FUNSPOT OWNER.

A reporter pushed a microphone into his face. "Mr. Spencer, is it true you're in talks to purchase Funspot back from Mr. Rodriguez?"

Doug Spencer smiled patiently. "No comment," he said. "I'll say only that these are tragic circumstances, but maybe everything will work out for the best."

The reporter sent it back to the anchorwoman, who quickly launched into another story about rabid raccoons or something. I'd stopped paying attention. "Doug Spencer?" I said to Frank.

He looked thoughtful. "Do you remember what Hector's wife said last night?" he asked.

I nodded. "'You forced that poor man to sell it to us,'" I replied. "She had to have been talking about this guy—this Doug Spencer."

"And if he was pressured into selling it, of course he'd want it back," Frank pointed out.

I took another long sip of coffee, considering. Could Doug Spencer have wanted Funspot back badly enough to take some very drastic actions?

My mom came tripping into the kitchen, shoving her toes into a very pointy-looking high heel. "No time for breakfast," she gasped. "I've got a showing in ten minutes. Last-minute New York people, but they seem really interested in the mansion on Juniper—"

Rrrrring. Rrrring!

She was cut off by the ringing of our landline.

The phone was right next to my mother, so she grabbed the receiver. "Hello?"

As the person on the other end spoke, her brow slowly furrowed. "Yes, they're here," she said. "I'm their mother. What is this about?" She glanced at Frank and me. "I see . . . I see. Hold on."

She pressed the receiver against her shoulder and turned to us. "It's some lawyer," she said, "representing somebody named Piperato. He says his clients are desperate to meet with you two."

She raised her eyebrows so high, they nearly hit her hairline. I knew what that expression meant. It meant, *What are you boys doing that lawyers are calling the house?*

Frank looked at me. "Tell him we want to hear what they have to say," he said. My mother shook her head and relayed the message.

"Maybe talking to them will give us some clues," Frank whispered to me.

I sure hoped so. Because I wasn't going to survive many more sleepless nights.

3 AWKWARD!

FRANK

SO WHAT DO YOU KNOW ABOUT DOUG Spencer?" I asked as we made the short drive to school.

Joe startled. I realized after I asked the question that he might have fallen asleep. He looked at me through hooded, red-rimmed eyes. "What?"

"Sorry. I asked you about Doug Spencer," I explained. "What do you know about him?"

Joe looked out the windshield at the gray, gloomy weather. His expression looked just as bleak. "Nothing," he said. "Nada. Diddly and squat. Why?"

I shrugged. "You were dating Daisy for a few weeks," I pointed out. "I thought maybe she'd mentioned him? Especially if Hector bought Funspot from him under some kind of duress."

Joe shook his head. "Daisy never mentioned him at all. I wish she had. I wish I had some idea what happened to her."

I'd just pulled into the BHS parking lot. I slid the car into a space and put it in park. Then I reached out and patted Joe's shoulder. "I know this must be tough for you, bro." Really, you just had to look at him to see that.

Joe nodded. "Thanks." He sighed, sitting up and grabbing his backpack. "Well, since Daisy's not around to ask, we're going to have to settle for the next best thing," he said.

I frowned. "Which is?"

Joe turned and looked at me. He was wearing a super-sleepy smirk. "Penelope Chung."

Penelope Chung is not exactly a huge fan of mine. The night the G-Force first opened, and we got to take its inaugural ride, Penelope was my setup "date." Let's just say she was not the Princess Kate to my Prince William. She was utterly bored by me and my science talk, and she made that completely clear.

But a case is a case, and clearly, it was more important to find out what happened to Daisy than for me to feel, well, like I was not something disgusting that Penelope had just stepped in. So I gamely approached her table with Joe that day at lunch.

“Hey, Penelope,” Joe said without preamble, barging right into the middle of a conversation Penelope and her friend Jamie King were having. “Can I ask you something?”

Penelope and Jamie looked up. Jamie, who we’d learned from questioning her the week before was a bit of a drama queen, looked stunned and horrified.

“Oh . . . em . . . gee,” she said, adopting that “mean girl” accent that every girl between the ages of thirteen and thirty seems to know how to do. “You guys . . . just no. This is, like, totally awkward.”

Joe looked at her, cocking an eyebrow. “Awkward?” he asked, like it was a foreign word he’d never heard before.

Jamie widened her blue eyes. “You *guys*. You know you can’t sit here, right? I know Daisy’s not here right now. But Joe, you and Daisy *broke up*.”

Joe made absolutely no response, except to look back at me. He looked exhausted. I got the feeling he was having serious trouble understanding what Jamie was talking about.

It was time for me to step up. “Actually, while I totally agree that it would be awkward for us to sit at your lunch table,” I said, giving Joe a pointed look, “we don’t want to. We just wanted to see if we could talk to Penelope for a second and ask her an important question. Okay?”

Jamie looked like she didn’t quite believe me, but she shrugged and turned back to her Cobb salad. “Whatever. I guess you’d have to ask *her*.”

Obviously. Which is what we were doing.

But I digress. Penelope was looking at the two of us like we'd just crawled out of a sewer. She didn't exactly look thrilled to talk to us. But she sighed and dropped her napkin on the table, then stood and faced us. "Okay. But let's make it quick."

Joe nodded and led the way to the far end of the cafeteria, where the uncool kids—like ourselves—usually ate. We settled down at a four-top table. Penelope sat reluctantly, looking around like uncoolness was a contagious disease.

Joe got right to the point. "We wanted to ask you about Doug Spencer," he said.

Penelope frowned. "The Funspot guy?"

I nodded. "The guy who sold Funspot to Hector. Did Daisy ever mention him?"

She sighed, looking off into the distance like she was trying to remember. "She told me that he didn't really want to sell Funspot," she said. "But he was running out of money. Her dad saw it as a business opportunity. He made Spencer an offer, but it was for less than he wanted."

Joe looked intrigued. "But he did sell it eventually?"

Penelope nodded. "He had to. He said he just couldn't make the park work in this economy. It needed too many repairs and stuff." She stuck her index finger in her mouth and started nibbling on the fingernail.

I glanced at Joe. "Did she ever meet him?" I asked Penelope.

It seemed clear that Spencer might have an ax to grind with Hector. But how would that lead him to Daisy? And how did this play into what the Piperato Brothers had done?

Penelope put her hand down and swallowed. She suddenly brightened, as if she'd just recalled something. "She met him a couple times," she said. "He came to the house to sign papers or something. She said he was really weird to her—giving her a lot of the side eye."

I was confused. "What does that mean?"

She let out a frustrated sigh. "You know. The side eye?" She turned so that she was facing ninety degrees away from me, then gave me a once-over out of the corner of her eye. Her eye traveled from the top of my head all the way down to my shoes. Then she turned back in her seat and looked at me dead on.

She gave me a *duh* kind of look. "The side eye is creepy. Definitely creepy. Wait a minute. . . ."

She trailed off, hostility sneaking back into her voice. Her eyes unfocused, and then suddenly she turned and glared at Joe.

"Are you asking because you two are investigating her disappearance?"

I glanced at my brother. "We . . . uh," was as far as I got.

"Yes," Joe told Penelope, "we're trying to figure out what happened to her."

Penelope's glare intensified. Her eyes flashed. "That's just great," she said snottily. "After all, you guys did such a great job of solving the G-Force case and keeping Daisy safe, right?"

Before either one of us could respond, Penelope jumped to her feet. Her eyes narrowed, and she fired this parting shot before she stomped off:

"Maybe if we're all lucky, this investigation will end in a murder!"

I gulped into the silence that followed Penelope's exit. Other uncool kids were looking over at us, no doubt curious what the Hardy Boys had done this time. But their reaction was nothing compared to Joe's. He was staring down at his hot lunch, stricken, like Penelope had ripped out his heart and stomped on it right in front of the whole student body.

I tried to make a joke. "Now that," I said, poking Joe in the shoulder, "was awkward!"

Joe looked up at me like I'd just run over his puppy. (Have I mentioned that I stink at making jokes?)

"Sorry," I said, softening my voice. "Listen, Joe, we'll get to the bottom of this. We always do."

Joe swallowed hard, pushing his tray away like he'd lost his appetite. "We'd better," he said.

Later that afternoon, I was shoving books from my locker into my backpack when a tiny piece of paper fluttered out. My heart quickened, remembering our recent investigation into the possible existence of a nasty criminal organization called the Red Arrow. When I picked up the paper, I was totally expecting to see the little triangle-with-legs doodle that was the Red Arrow's symbol, implying that I'd been marked for further punishment. But instead what I saw was an angry message scrawled in black marker:

STOP LOOKING FOR DAISY OR YOU'LL REGRET IT.

THE UGLY TRUTH

4

JOE

I STARED AT THE NOTE FRANK HAD GIVEN ME as he pulled out of our school parking lot and started the drive to the Seaside County Jail.

"Penelope," I said, searching the block letters for any resemblance to her cute, girly handwriting. "It has to be. Right?"

Frank shrugged. "Who else knows that we're investigating?"

I considered. "Chief Olaf kind of knows. Hector. Maybe Luke."

"It could be Luke," Frank pointed out.

I was doubtful. "And he snuck into our school to slip this note in your locker—when he should have been at Dalton Academy?" I paused, then added, "After we just told Penelope? And she was clearly upset? And she goes to our school?"

He sighed. "I agree, Penelope makes the most sense," he said. "I just think we should keep an open mind. We talked to all kinds of people while we were trying to find Kelly and Luke. Or maybe someone's figured out what we're doing who we don't even know about."

Well, that was comforting.

We rode in silence for a few minutes. I looked at my brother's profile as he drove, and I couldn't quite tell what he was thinking.

I figured I had to say it.

"We can't stop investigating."

Frank stopped at a stoplight and looked over at me, surprised. "Of course not," he said. "We have to find Daisy."

I settled back in my seat, relieved.

Ninety percent of the time Frank and I think alike. I was glad this was one of those times.

The Seaside County Jail is a place the Hardy Boys know well. We've sent tons of crooks there. So we greeted our friends in security and wasted no time in being led to the big shared visitation lounge. It was a loud, cold room, the size of our school's gym, filled with tables where inmates could speak with their visitors. A few minutes after we sat down, I caught sight of the Piperato Brothers being led in.

Greg and Derek Piperato looked very different without their usual hipster outfits. Without a zoot suit and a fedora, Greg's handlebar mustache looked a little ridiculous, especially balanced against the bright orange of a prisoner's jumpsuit. The Piperatos had been in jail, awaiting trial for fraud and kidnapping. The elaborate hoax they'd dreamed up to gain publicity for the G-Force had bitten them back, big-time.

Also missing was the brothers' usual affected attitude. As he was being led in, Greg Piperato (always the nicer of the two) looked at Frank and me like he was a starving man, and we were the last drumstick in all of America.

Or something like that. I don't know, I was tired.

"Thank you so much for coming," Greg said as he and his brother slipped into their chairs across the table. "We were afraid you wouldn't. We know we haven't, ah, exactly gotten off on the right foot?" He chuckled awkwardly.

"You constructed an elaborate hoax that caused a lot of people a lot of fear and heartbreak, all to get publicity for an amusement ride, and we caught you," Frank replied drily. "So yeah, we're not best buds."

Derek's desperate eyes clouded over with anger. "You self-righteous little worm! I—"

But Greg held up his hand, and Derek was instantly silenced. He stared down into his lap, pouting.

"As I was saying," Greg went on, "I don't think we've

really gotten to know each other." He paused and tried to catch Derek's eye, giving him a hopeful look. Derek nodded. "If you knew us, you'd know there's no way we could do what we've been accused of."

I wasn't convinced. "There has to be a way," I replied, "because you left a digital trail. What about all the e-mails from you to Luke and Kelly, telling them how to fake their disappearances?"

Derek jumped in his seat, and Greg held up his hand again. Derek sighed and turned back to his lap.

"We didn't send those," Greg insisted.

I looked at my brother. Hmm. Of course it made sense for Greg to lie to us in this situation. But his calm manner—along with the utter certainty in his voice—had me intrigued.

I could tell Frank was feeling the same. "Prove it," he said simply.

Derek sighed again. "We can't," he said.

Greg held up a finger. "My brother is right. We can't prove that we didn't send those e-mails. I can only tell you the truth, and hope that you believe me. Remember, legally, we do not have to prove our innocence. The state has to prove our guilt—beyond a reasonable doubt."

He had a point. I looked at Frank, who nodded slowly.

"Tell me about the e-mails," I said.

Greg leaned closer. "It would not have been difficult for someone to hack into our e-mail," he explained. "We love engineering, but we've never been computer people. We shared the same password for our accounts, which was, I'm ashamed to admit, 'password.'"

Frank groaned. Being a bit of a computer geek, I'm sure he was personally pained by such lazy password choosing.

"It doesn't even have a number," he muttered, shaking his head.

"Exactly." Greg waited for Frank to meet his eyes, then turned and looked me straight in the eye too. "Anyone with basic computer literacy could have hacked into our e-mail and sent those messages. And if this were someone close to the case—someone who, say, was trying to mislead the authorities . . ."

This was all sounding a little too reasonable. "But Luke and Kelly think you did it," I pointed out. "The whole time, they believed they were being instructed by you—and, after they had 'disappeared,' cared for by you."

Derek suddenly pounded on the table. "Lies!"

Greg turned and gave him a slow-burning glare. "Derek," he said, and his brother seemed to calm down before our eyes. He shook his head, frowning down at the table again.

Greg then turned to us. "Those children never saw us," he pointed out. "It was Cal, the ride operator, who was transporting them and bringing them food. He has since disappeared, so he can't tell anyone who was truly behind the crime."

All true. Cal Nevins, the gruff ride operator and childhood friend of Hector's, had disappeared as soon as we made it clear that we had reason to suspect him. And both Luke and Kelly said it was Cal who'd cared for them in the wake of their "disappearances"—until he disappeared himself.

I let out a slow sigh. I hate, hate, hate catching the wrong guy.

But had we done it this time?

Greg looked from Frank to me, seeming to read the uncertainty in our faces. "I'd also like you to think about why we contacted you today," he said.

I raised an eyebrow. Was he serious? "To get out of jail?" I asked sarcastically. "Yes, I wonder why you're saying you're innocent? How unusual!"

Greg didn't have any visible reaction. "We only get out of jail if you catch the real criminal," he said. "We understand the criminal justice system well enough to know that. So there's no benefit to us in contacting you unless we're really innocent."

I was still trying to wrap my mind around that when Derek spoke again. This time his voice was hoarse and serious.

"That young girl, Daisy, disappeared last night," he said.

Frank nodded. "She disappeared on the ride, just like Luke and Kelly."

Derek's eyes widened. "But we are in here," he pointed out. "Don't you see? Whoever's behind these disappearances is still out there. While we rot away with the drug dealers and scum of the earth, the true criminal is running loose, causing real harm."

Frank shook his head. "But Daisy's disappearance is different," he said. "She was never in the little crawlspace under the ride. It sounds like this is a different crime, for a different criminal."

"Or is it a different crime from the same criminal?" Greg asked, tilting his head. "Maybe it's not a different person—maybe it's the same person, now moved into a different phase of whatever terrible thing he has planned."

A chill went down my spine when he said that. A different phase of whatever terrible thing . . . There was no denying that a person who'd faked Kelly's and Luke's disappearances as some kind of prologue to Daisy's real disappearance—and whatever else he had planned—was a lot more sinister, and scarier, than some bozo committing a copycat crime for attention.

I considered this for a moment before meeting Greg's eyes.

"We behaved inappropriately," he said. "We realize that now. We took advantage of the disappearances. We were callous and cruel. We tried to use a real crime to gain publicity for our creation." He stopped and leaned closer to me. "But she could get hurt," he said. "It's crucial that you understand the ugly truth of this crime. It isn't a copycat crime. I fear it's something far darker." He paused. "Do you understand?"

I glanced at Frank. He was staring at the table, deep

inside his own mind. I knew he, too, was turning what the Piperatos had told us over and over, trying to make sense of it.

"We understand," I said.

I wondered where Daisy was as we walked out of the jail into the startlingly bright midafternoon sunlight. I wondered so hard my head hurt and I couldn't focus on anything else. *It's such a waste,* I remember thinking. *I can put so much thought and brainpower into trying to save her, and still not save her. I can wish myself into knots hoping that she's safe, and she might not be safe.*

The Piperatos' message hadn't made me feel any better, or any closer to finding the person who'd taken Daisy. Instead it made the world feel much bigger and darker, and much harder to understand, than it had just moments before we'd stepped into the jail.

Frank and I do what we do because we want, in an unsentimental way, to make the world a better place.

But what if we hadn't this time?

What if we'd made it worse?

"I believe them," Frank said, suddenly stopping dead a few yards away from our car. I could tell he'd been thinking this over since we'd left the visitation room.

"I think I believe them too," I said, sighing.

Frank nodded. We kept walking to the car, both still lost in thought, and Frank unlocked the doors and started to climb in just as I pulled my door open and saw something that sent raw terror blooming through my gut.

"Frank!" I screamed. "Stop! Get back!"

In the driver's seat, coiled like a snail's shell, but with a hissing, toothy head protruding, was a live rattlesnake.

5 JUNGLE FUN!

FRANK

I DIDN'T THINK I COULD GET ANY MORE SHAKEN up after hearing what the Piperato Brothers had to say about Daisy's disappearance.

But it's funny how finding a live rattlesnake in your car really wakes you up and forces you into action.

"HOLY . . . ," I managed, staring at the slithering, hissing beast that coiled precisely where I'd been about to slide my butt just seconds ago.

"Close the door, Frank!" Joe yelled from the passenger side. "Close it!"

He was right. Of course he was right. I slammed the door on the reptile invader and backed away.

"Look!" Joe said. He was pointing at the windshield, where a small white note fluttered, pinned facedown by the left wiper. It took me a minute to be brave enough to approach the car again, but I reminded myself that the snake was inside, the note was outside. I grabbed the tiny paper and backed away again.

"What does it say?" Joe asked, running around the car to join me on the driver's side.

I looked down, then held it up so he could read:

I TOLD YOU TO STOP LOOKING.

Joe stared at the note, then stepped back and shook his head. "Well. Awesome."

A few hours later we were back at the Bayport PD, having spent a couple of hours dealing with the cops, then animal control. Our slithery friend had been taken into custody and examined, while animal control officers searched missing animal reports. It turned out that our unwelcome visitor was none other than Poky, an elderly rattlesnake that lived at Funspot's long-running Jungle Fun! exhibit. According to his handlers, Poky was a really super-nice rattlesnake who was enjoying living out his golden years on a steady diet of mice and occasional cuddling. He wasn't super interested in biting people.

I still did not like him. And I really did not like whoever had stuck him in my car.

Officer Fernandez led us through reception and into

Chief Olaf's office, which was empty. I looked at Joe and sighed. When Fernandez responded to our call, he'd been reluctant to let us go after making our initial report, claiming that there were some "things we need to discuss" back at the station. Apparently these things needed to be discussed with the chief. This day was just getting better and better.

Fernandez told us to sit and then said he'd go get the chief. A couple of minutes later Chief Olaf came back alone. He closed the door and walked over behind his desk, looking at the two of us with a serious expression.

"Boys," he said. "I take it you survived the rattlesnake attack?"

I tried to smile. "It turns out Poky isn't much of an attacker."

The chief nodded. "Nevertheless," he said. "I was told that there was also a threatening note, the text of which was . . ." He paused and pulled a piece of lined paper out of his pocket. "'I told you to stop looking.'"

He looked from the paper to us.

I looked at Joe.

I wasn't really sure what to say.

Chief Olaf let out a long, slow sigh. "Boys, it sounds like you two might be doing some investigating. And someone is clearly aware of that fact and has started threatening you."

Joe cleared his throat and sat up. "We've had our eyes and ears open, sure," he said. "But we've been careful so far."

The chief nodded and looked from Joe to me. His frank

stare was a little unnerving. He sighed again. "Even so, for your own safety, I'm going to ask you to suspend your investigation."

But there are just some things Hardys can't do. For us, not sleuthing was like not living.

Especially in this case . . .

Joe looked upset. He squirmed in his chair and then said, "Chief?"

Olaf looked at him patiently. "Yes, Joe?"

Joe sighed, clearly frustrated. "It's just . . . we really care about Daisy. And we really want to try to find her. Isn't that, maybe, sort of understandable?"

I looked at the chief, curious how he would react. He touched his temples and looked down.

"I could understand that," he said, looking up to meet Joe's eyes. "But boys, I need you to listen to me. You're being threatened. We know that things aren't always perfect in this town. You need to leave this case to the professionals—for your own good."

Joe frowned. He seemed to listen to the chief, but he clearly didn't like it. "But—" he said, squirming again.

"For your own good," Chief Olaf repeated. He shook his head. "Look, you boys were lucky this time. But I don't want to have to explain to your parents why you were attacked by rabid dogs or pushed off a cliff! Are we clear?"

Joe sighed. I caught his eye, and subtly nodded.

"We're clear," Joe said, obviously not happy about it.

"We're clear," I echoed.

Olaf nodded. "Good," he said. "Now, I believe Officer Fernandez has some paperwork for you to sign regarding the rattlesnake. After that, I've been told your car has been examined and deemed safe, so you can head home."

We stood and followed the chief out of his office and down the hall toward Fernandez's desk, near the reception area. The officer looked from Olaf to us and nodded. "Boys," he said, pulling a manila folder off his desk. "I just need your John Hancock on a few forms, and you're free to go."

Olaf gave us a quick wave and disappeared back toward his office. Joe and I sat at Fernandez's desk and quickly started passing the forms back and forth. I didn't know about Joe, but I was ready to be home. I hoped Aunt Trudy had worked up some kind of super-comforting comfort food for dinner.

Fernandez watched us sign. "So," he said in a low voice, too low to be heard by anyone else in the office, "you boys been checking out the Funspot case?"

I looked at Joe, wondering if we should share any information with Fernandez. And I had no idea why he was asking.

Joe met my eye and furrowed his brow. "We might have heard some things," he said noncommittally, signing away.

"Hmm," Fernandez said, looking around, then back to his computer. We signed a few more forms before he spoke again. "You find out anything?" he whispered.

Joe stopped signing and looked at me. I had no idea what to say. Should we—

"Stop it! You're hurting me! I said I can walk myself!"

I started at the familiar voice. Could it be?

"I want to talk to my lawyer! I know my rights!"

I looked up at the door. Two big, burly officers were struggling to lead in a cuffed—and angry—Hector Rodriguez!

Joe had looked up now and his mouth dropped open, the pen falling from his hand to Fernandez's desk. "Is that . . . ?"

Fernandez looked up and grinned. "Yup. That's your buddy Hector Rodriguez."

Joe ducked a little, and I followed suit. I don't know why, but I didn't want Hector to know we were witnessing this.

"What did he do?" I asked.

The officer sniffed. "He's innocent until proven guilty," he said, glancing at his computer and clicking around. "But it says here he was brought in on an assault charge. Guy says he showed up at his door and attacked him."

"Who was the guy?" Joe asked.

Fernandez clicked again. "Some guy named Douglas Spencer."

CRIES FOR HELP

6

JOE

AND WE'RE BACK AT DOUG SPENCER," Frank said as we pulled into our driveway. The lights were on in the kitchen, sending out a comforting yellow glow, and at the sight of them I really couldn't wait to have a nice hot dinner and then climb into bed. I was exhausted, and I needed a break from all the horrible thoughts that kept swirling about Daisy and what might have happened to her.

"But we know next to nothing about him," I pointed out, opening up my door and climbing out of the car. "Except what Penelope said."

"Which was what?" Frank asked, looking thoughtful. I couldn't blame him for forgetting. Lunch seemed like a million years ago.

"He didn't want to sell Funspot, and he was giving Daisy creepy looks when he came by the house," I replied. *Side eye,* she'd called it. I really had no idea what to make of it, still. Was it a sign that Doug Spencer was dangerous? Or were his looks just innocent curiosity?

Frank nodded as we walked toward the house.

"So what do we do?" I asked. I was almost too tired to think about it.

Frank smiled. "We do what we always do when we have a little bit of a clue, but not enough of a clue to know what to do."

When I looked at him wonderingly, he went on, "We do an Internet search."

"Why would Hector attack Doug?" I asked as we settled down in front of Frank's computer. Aunt Trudy, God bless her, was downstairs putting the finishing touches on an organic butternut squash lasagna. The smell—sort of sweet, sort of cheesy—was like a warm blanket wrapping me up in homey comfort.

Frank opened up his Internet browser. "Good question," he said as his favorite Internet search site came up. "We've been thinking about grudges Doug might have against Hector. But why would Hector want to attack Doug?"

I swallowed. "It had to involve Daisy," I said. "We know Hector, and he's not a violent guy. The only reason I can think of that Hector would try to hurt someone is to defend his child."

Frank frowned, looking pensive. "Hector does have a criminal record, remember," he said. "He may not be a violent guy, but he wasn't exactly a choirboy in his youth. Remember how he had a few run-ins with the law?"

I sighed. "He seemed so eager to leave that behind, though." I shook my head. "I think it's Daisy. I feel like Hector must have had some reason to suspect Doug of having something to do with her disappearance."

Frank clicked on the search box and typed in "Doug Spencer, Bayport." "Let's see," he said, and clicked on the search button.

It took hours to wade through all the results. First we had to sort out the hits that referred to our Doug Spencer—the former owner of Funspot—and not Doug Spencer, the World War II veteran, or Doug Spencer, the young hermit crab enthusiast. Then we broke for dinner. Then we came back to filter out the ones that had bad, or irrelevant, or repetitive information.

Most of what we found had to do with Funspot. Doug Spencer had owned the park for almost thirty years. There were tons of photos and nostalgia sites for the Funspot of our youth, the well-kept, cute amusement park that I could remember our parents taking Frank and me to visit. But one link led Frank to an interesting discovery.

"'Douglas Spencer, 45 Lincoln Road, Bayport,'" he read. "And here's his phone number."

I nodded. "Seems worth a ride over there," I suggested, even though I was having trouble keeping my eyes open.

"But wait—look," said Frank, jumping back to the search results and scrolling down to a different one. It was the website for the local Kiwanis Club, a public service club that met once a month. Doug Spencer was listed as an active member.

"Look at the meeting time," Frank whispered, pointing.

It was the second Saturday of every month—which would be tomorrow.

"If we wait till tomorrow morning, we can check out his house when he's not home," I said.

Frank nodded. "I think that's the way to go," he replied. "Though I guess you could argue, if he really is keeping Daisy in his closet, he might not show up for the Kiwanis meeting."

I shivered. I knew Frank was kidding, but I hated to think of Daisy being kept in a closet.

My brother glanced at me, and his brow furrowed with sympathy. "Sorry, Joe. Look, let's both get some sleep. We need it. Then we'll leave the house tomorrow by eight thirty. Sound good?"

I nodded. "It's a plan," I said, dragging myself off the edge of Frank's bed and shuffling toward my room. "G'night."

"Night," Frank called after me. Once I was in the hall, he added, "Joe?"

"Yeah?"

His voice took on a tone of certainty. "We'll find her," he said.

I gulped. I wanted to believe my brother, but I just wasn't sure. "See you in the morning."

I thought I'd be too keyed up to sleep again, but I guess my body knew better: Within seconds of my head hitting the pillow, I fell into a deep sleep. I awoke with the sun streaming through my window and a puddle of drool on my pillow. I slowly rose up, stretched, and looked around. I couldn't remember dreaming at all—for which I was grateful.

I checked my phone: seven thirty. Just enough time to shower, throw on clothes, and wolf down some of Aunt Trudy's steel-cut oatmeal before we ran out the door. I grabbed some jeans and a T-shirt and stumbled into the hall. Frank's bedroom door was open, so I poked my head in.

"Hey," I called. My brother was sitting at his computer, peering at the screen, fully dressed. I wondered how long he'd been up.

"Hey," he replied, turning around. "It looks like Doug Spencer doesn't live luxuriously." He pointed to the screen, where his map website showed an image of 45 Lincoln Road. I stepped inside to take a closer look.

The house was small, with white-painted clapboard that was flaking off in places, and a roof that seemed to sink in. The yard was small but tidy. In the background I could see the house behind, which was in worse condition, junk littering the yard.

"Strange," I murmured. "I know Hector paid less than Doug wanted for Funspot, but it should have been enough for Doug to buy a nice house, at least."

"Hmm." Frank closed the browser. "Well, let's see what we can find. You go take a shower. I'll heat us up some oatmeal."

We think alike.

A little over an hour later we pulled onto Lincoln Road. Bayport is a pretty standard northeastern town: There are ritzy parts and not-so-ritzy parts, but mostly in-between parts. This was a not-so-ritzy part. Lincoln Road sat between a line of seedy motels and strip malls and the river. It was lined with small houses, all of which looked like they'd seen better days.

Frank suddenly pulled over to the side of the road and turned off the engine. "Look," he said, pointing to the house we'd seen on his computer: 45 Lincoln Road.

A nondescript silver sedan was pulling out. As we watched, it backed into the street and then drove off in the direction we'd just come from. As it passed, I recognized the driver as Doug Spencer. He stared straight ahead, a vague smile on his face. He didn't seem to notice us.

When the car turned left and disappeared toward the main drag, Frank and I looked at each other.

"It's on," I said.

Frank pulled the car closer to number 45 and parked. We climbed out cautiously, looking all around us, but the neighborhood still appeared to be mostly asleep.

We glanced at each other once more and then darted up the path that led to number 45.

The house had a tiny porch that we eagerly climbed onto. The house was quiet, and I pressed my ear to the door. Nothing. There was a small window to the right, and I peered in, but saw nothing except for a totally normal living room, neatly arranged, television off. Photos of smiling children were arranged on the far wall.

"Come on," whispered Frank.

He led me down off the porch, and we crept around to the left. Another window looked into what seemed to be a small office—I could see bookshelves near the ceiling—but without the porch, we were too short to see in.

"I'll boost you up," Frank suggested after a few seconds. He crouched down on the ground and made a stirrup out of his hands. I stuck my foot into it, and he lifted me up as much as he could.

"Oof! Aunt Trudy's been feeding you too well," he gasped.

"That goes for both of us," I hissed back as I grabbed onto the sill and managed to pull myself up enough to see inside.

Sure enough, it was a small, neat home office. An older computer sat on a wooden desk, attached to a printer. More framed photos of the same smiling children were scattered around the desk and the walls. One little girl of two or three with very short blond hair posed in a cowboy hat, giggling at the camera. There was also a set of older twins posed in holiday finery. On the far wall I saw that Spencer had framed some old postcards of Funspot, dating back (it looked like) to the 1950s. On that same wall was a framed photo of Spencer himself with someone dressed like Giggly the Funosaur, Funspot's official mascot.

Suddenly a sound erupted from the other side of the house: "WAHHH . . ."

Frank jumped and suddenly lost his grip. I went plummeting down, my fingernails scraping the clapboard as I slid. It wasn't far—only a few feet—but it was enough to get some splinters and land hard on my right hip.

The sound came again. It seemed to pierce the sleepy weekend-morning air. "WAHHHH!"

Icy dread crept down my spine as I pulled myself to my feet. What was that?

I looked at my brother. Frank's expression seemed to ask the same question.

"Around back," he said simply.

I nodded. We wasted no time in bolting toward the back of the house, only to find a tall chain-link fence that surrounded the backyard.

"Crap," I whispered.

Frank cast a disapproving glance at me. "This fence is

no match for the Hardy Boys!" he pointed out, scrambling halfway up in seconds.

"I know," I said, climbing up behind him. "OW! It's just, my hip is still sore."

I checked the backyard for any sign of a dog. Our investigative experience had taught us that fences like this usually contained a dog. Most often a large, sharp-toothed, ill-tempered dog. I patted the plastic bag I'd tucked into my shirt pocket. It contained a fresh pork bone from the local butcher, which was usually enough to make friends with even the nastiest dog. I always come prepared when we "visit" a strange house.

The backyard appeared empty. I scrambled up behind Frank, trying to put most of my weight on my noninjured hip. It still hurt, though. Ouch. Ouch. Ouch.

"Here we are," Frank said, gesturing around a totally nondescript backyard. Neatly cut grass, some weeds around the edges. A slightly beat-up table with two chairs. And lots of bushes.

Big, heavy evergreen bushes flanked the back of the house, broken only by a short set of stairs that led down from a back door. The bushes made it difficult to see anything.

Frank crept closer and peered down into the bush on the right.

"WAHHH!"

The sound came again, and it made me jump. I said what I knew both of us were thinking: "It sounds like someone crying."

Frank pointed into the bush. "There are windows almost flush with the ground line. It must be a basement. It sounds like the crying is coming from there."

I crept closer behind him. Frank reached out to pull some branches of the bush apart, then yelped and yanked his hand back. "Thorns!"

"Great," I muttered. Frank sighed and reached inside his jacket to produce two pairs of work gloves. We've gotten enough scrapes and cuts in our day to know to come prepared.

He handed a pair to me. "Let's do this."

I put on the gloves and grabbed a branch. Peering inside, I could see that there were a good eight feet of bush before we got to the house. My stomach sank, but I knew we didn't really have a choice. We had to find out what was happening in that basement. Had to.

Frank pushed the bushes aside farther and stepped in. "Ow!" he said almost immediately. "It got me on the face!"

I looked into the uninviting, thorn-encrusted branches and sighed. I stepped in behind him—and immediately felt sharp thorns scraping against my side when my shirt got caught on a branch. "Ow," I said. "I hate this bush!"

"This bush is the worst," Frank agreed. "It's possessed by demons or something. OUCH!"

"WAHHHH!"

The sound was much closer now. It made my blood run cold and reminded me that there was no time to waste. In front of me a huge cluster of branches twined together, making it hard to see what lay beyond. I grabbed the knot in the middle with my work gloves and pulled it toward me, revealing a tiny space—

"AAAAAAAAAUUUGHHH!" Something small, orange, and *very* angry launched itself at my face and dug in, scratching me worse than the bush could have hoped for.

"WAHHHH!" the evil beast screeched.

I stumbled backward through the bush, hitting every thorn and branch that I had so carefully pushed aside just seconds before. I had to get away from that thing. Suddenly I heard Frank roar—

"NOOOOOOOOOOOO!"

—and I heard a sound like *Ssssss!*

Then a horrible stench filled the air.

As I collapsed backward onto the lawn, I saw something black and white stream past and disappear through a hole beneath the fence. After a moment, the orange beast dislodged its claws from my cheeks and followed, letting out a nasty "WAHHH!" in parting.

I lay on my back and looked at the sky. All was silent now. Frank stumbled out of the bushes, groaning. He smelled awful.

"What happened?" I moaned.

Frank collapsed beside me. The stench intensified, and I actually had to climb back up to my feet to get away from him. My hip throbbed again.

"It was a skunk," he said wonderingly, shaking his head. "It was a skunk fighting with a feral cat. The cat was what we heard. That sound like crying."

I frowned, looking at my brother as he slowly got to his feet. "I don't know if I can ride home with you," I said.

He glared at me. "Great. Then walk."

"Maybe I could get a cab," I murmured. I was serious. Frank plus skunk was the worst thing I had ever smelled.

"Let's take a quick look around," he growled at me. "Then we'll get out of here. This was a bad idea."

I wasn't so sure it was a bad idea, so much as we had been bested by the elements. It just goes to show, no matter how much you prepare as an investigator, you can't prepare for the unexpected.

I sensed from Frank's expression, however, that he wasn't looking for a philosophical discussion.

We peered in windows, pressed our ears against them. It was all the same, though: ordinary. No sign of Daisy. No sign that she had ever been there.

So why had Hector attacked Doug Spencer?

Frank swiped at his eyes.

"Are you crying?" I asked. I wasn't judging. I would cry if I smelled like him too.

He stopped and glared at me. "No. The . . . skunk stink is getting in my eyes and irritating them. You'd better drive home."

I noted that he was ignoring how I'd said maybe I could

get a cab, and I decided that was probably for the best. "All right," I said with a sigh.

Frank tossed me the keys. Oh, they smelled. I tried to ignore it as I stepped up to the back door and pressed my nose one last time against the small window that led into the kitchen.

I heard a sudden yelp from my brother, but before I could react, a gruff voice growled into my ear, "Enjoying the view?"

Then a hand grabbed the back of my collar and threw me down the steps onto the ground.

7 KIDS TODAY

FRANK

THE MAN THREW OPEN A GATE IN THE fence and crashed in before I could warn Joe. I managed a kind of pitiful sound—a yelp, maybe—before the man growled something in my brother's ear and tossed him down the two steps to the ground.

As the man turned to look down at Joe, I got my first good look at him.

"Doug Spencer?" I croaked.

As Joe groaned, Spencer held up a cell phone. "My home security system texts me when there's been a disturbance," he said. "When it said someone was scratching at the windows, I assumed it was those darned feral cats that always hang around. Instead I find two nearly grown men skulking around my backyard. What's your explanation?" He frowned, looking us up and down. "You two don't look like the typical neighborhood hooligans. Though you smell terrible." He wrinkled his nose at me.

"I had a run-in with a skunk," I began, then immediately realized that probably wasn't the explanation he was looking for. "Mr. Spencer, I'm so sorry. It's just—we thought—we heard that—"

I broke off, realizing that there was probably no explanation that would seem reasonable to him.

Joe struggled to a sitting position and winced. "We're friends of Daisy Rodriguez," he said. "And we heard—well, we know that—we know her father was here last night."

Spencer made a noise that sounded like a growl. He turned away, then sighed.

"That poor man," he said finally. "I wouldn't wish what happened with his daughter on anybody."

I glanced at Joe. "Do you know why Hector was here?" I asked, figuring that getting right to the point would be appreciated.

Spencer shrugged. "Do I know? Yes. Do I understand it? No." He paused, curling his lip. "He said he'd been getting strange e-mails from me. E-mails claiming that I knew where Daisy was. But I never sent any such thing."

I looked at Joe, and he nodded slightly. E-mails. So much in this case was coming down to e-mails—first from the Piperatos, though they claimed not to have sent those, and now from Doug Spencer.

"Sir," I said, "I don't mean to be disrespectful, but . . . Can you prove it?"

Spencer turned and glared at me. For a second I regretted my words, thinking he was seriously going to hit me. But then he softened. "Guess you must care about that girl," he muttered, and shook his head. "The police have been here and looked all over my computers. The e-mails he got didn't come from this house, that's for sure. The account wasn't one I'd even heard of. Only thing I can think of is someone opened it in my name."

Joe looked thoughtful. "Mr. Spencer, this might be a weird question, but do you have any enemies?"

Spencer laughed, a dry sound. "Enemies?" he asked. "No. I've been living in this same neighborhood for fifty years. I owned Funspot for almost thirty, and though I wished I'd kept it up better, I always felt good knowing that I'd brought lots of kids happiness. The only person I argued with recently is Hector Rodriguez, because I don't think he gave me a fair price for that park."

I cocked my head. "We heard on the news you were thinking of buying it back," I said.

Spencer nodded. His expression changed, and he looked almost wistful. "I sure would have liked to," he said. "But my accountant said it's impossible."

Joe glanced at the house. "What about the money Hector

paid you?" he asked. He wasn't saying it, but I knew he was thinking that the money hadn't gone into a new house or car. "I'm guessing he'd take less than that, under the circumstances."

Spencer shrugged, looking sad now. "Doesn't much matter. My little granddaughter, Tanya . . . She has leukemia. Half the money from Funspot went toward her treatment. I can't pull together enough to make what Hector's asking. And even if I could, I'm getting too old. For thirty years, that park took every one of my waking moments. I loved running it. But those days are over." He paused, and his mouth settled into a small smile. "Now I have plenty of time to read, go to Kiwanis meetings." He laughed. "And spend time with my grandchildren, which is what I really care about."

Joe nodded respectfully. "How's Tanya doing?" he asked gently.

Spencer smiled. "Better," he said. "I hope we have many more years to spend together. And I hope we'll get along when she's a teenager like you boys." He paused, and his face darkened. "The other thing about Funspot . . . If I'm being honest, that whole Death Ride thing disturbed me. The way kids were flocking there to go on some ride they thought might hurt them." He shook his head. "I'm just not sure I understand kids today."

I looked at my brother. "Honestly, sir . . . I'm not sure we do either."

Spencer looked at the house, then turned back to us. "Well, boys, if we're all square here, I would appreciate it if you got off my lawn."

Fair enough. "Of course, sir," Joe said. He held out his hand, and Spencer shook it. "Sorry again."

I held out my hand too, but Spencer just looked at it. "I think I'd rather not," he said.

Oh, right. I stank. "No problem, sir. Have a nice weekend."

Spencer held the gate open, and Joe and I scrambled through. We took the walk back to our car in silence.

Once Joe had unlocked the doors and we'd climbed in, I spoke. "That wasn't our shining hour."

Joe snorted. "Ugh. Oh man, you really stink." He opened all the windows, then pulled into the street.

"So what do we know?" I asked. The neighborhood seemed to be waking up; I saw a young guy in a hoodie, the hood pulled up, darting down the sidewalk. There was no traffic, so Joe made a quick left back to the main drag, and made an easy right.

Joe sighed. "Not enough?" he said. "Okay, it's looking more likely that the Piperatos didn't do it. Whoever did do it really wants us to stop investigating."

"Right," I said. Our run-in with Poky the rattlesnake had made that more than clear. "And whoever did it seems to have access to Funspot, even though it's been closed ever since Daisy disappeared," I pointed out, thinking of Poky being removed from the Jungle Fun! exhibit.

"Whoever did it created a fake e-mail account for Doug Spencer to implicate him," Joe added.

I sighed. It was frustrating how none of the things we knew seemed to be related.

The traffic light in front of us flashed from green to yellow, and I saw Joe move his foot to the brake. We were going pretty fast—it was the main drag, after all—but weirdly, the car didn't slow.

"Joe," I said, concerned. "Hit the brake!"

"I am," Joe said, pumping the pedal now. But the car didn't slow at all. The traffic light turned red as we hurtled toward the intersection. And suddenly I saw the one other car out this early on a Saturday morning—a huge Express Delivery truck!

Joe screamed. I leaned forward, bracing myself against the dashboard. There was nothing we could do.

The truck was speeding toward the intersection—right at us!

GETTING REAL 8

JOE

IT SEEMED TO BE HAPPENING IN SLOW MOTION, but I knew it was anything but. We sped into the intersection, unable to stop. The truck was hurtling toward us now, and I could see the driver's expression change when he realized we weren't stopping: First it was confusion, then anger, then very quickly, fear.

His mouth opened in a scream that matched my own. I grabbed the wheel, and then suddenly something came back to me. I pictured myself in driver's ed with Coach Gerther, the unair-conditioned room sweltering in the summer heat, one of the countless gruesome videos used to terrify teenagers into driving responsibly playing on the ancient television.

Coach Gerther suddenly paused the video (yes, video—this

film was from the 1980s at the latest) and held up the remote. "What would you do in this situation?" he asked. "Your brakes fail. You can't stop. What now?"

"Put the car in neutral, turn the wheel, and try to steer onto an upgrade," I whispered now, scrambling for the gearshift.

"What?" Frank screamed.

I grabbed the gearshift and shoved with all my might until the car was in neutral. The engine noise quieted, and as I turned the wheel, we spun out of the truck's path. On the opposite corner was a pancake restaurant with a steep circular driveway. I pulled in, the car slowing as the upgrade became steeper. Finally, just before the crest of the driveway, we crept to a stop, and I put on the emergency brake to prevent us from sliding backward.

"Wow," said Frank. It was the first time he'd spoken since I'd shifted into neutral.

"Thank you, Coach Gerther," I murmured.

Frank shook his head. "Unbelievable." He reached out to touch the windshield, pausing at a small piece of paper that flapped in the late-morning breeze. "What's that?"

I shrugged. Frank put down his window and reached around to grab it. He pulled it through and flipped it over. Angry block letters were printed on the other side.

YOU'RE STUBBORN. I TOLD YOU TO STOP LOOKING. NOW IT GETS REAL.

• • •

"Joe, are you ready?"

I looked up at Frank, who stood in my open doorway. I was dressed, my backpack packed, but was I ready? It was Monday, our first day back at school since our brakes had been cut. One day after we'd been given a major chewing out by Chief Olaf at the police station.

Dad had insisted on taking us down yesterday to report that someone had cut our brakes. We'd conveniently left the note out of our account to Dad, but Chief Olaf caught on immediately.

"Fenton," he said with a big smile, "is it okay if I meet with the boys privately to catch them up on some cases I know they have an interest in?"

Dad looked surprised—the Bayport PD is not exactly in the habit of debriefing us—but quickly agreed and left Olaf's office. Once the door was shut and we could hear his footsteps fading down the hall, the chief leaned across his desk toward us.

"What else?" he said simply.

I glanced at Frank. We didn't even bother pretending we didn't know what he was talking about.

"There was a note," Frank admitted, pulling it out of his pocket and handing it to the chief.

Chief Olaf huffed and looked down at it. "Same handwriting as last time," he said.

I nodded. "We're pretty sure it's the same person, sir."

Chief Olaf looked up at me and flashed his teeth in a sarcastic smile. "Are you?" he asked. "Well, I suppose that's what makes you the Hardy Boys." He threw the note down on his desk and shook his head. I shot Frank a slightly frightened look. Was the chief losing his patience? Did he suspect that we hadn't stopped looking into Daisy's disappearance?

The chief stared down at his desk for a moment, then looked up at us. "Boys," he said, in a voice quiet enough that we had to lean forward to hear him, "I cannot tell you how serious I am being right now. This is not a game anymore. Do you understand? This thing you're doing where you see how much you can get away with before someone kills you—you're getting dangerously close to the end. Get it?"

We just stared at him. Honestly, I had no idea what to say. I usually rely on Frank in instances such as these, but his jaw was hanging open.

"The Daisy Rodriguez case is taking all my manpower," Chief Olaf went on. "Whoever's threatening you has made clear that this isn't a game to them. And I simply don't have the personnel to send a car to follow you around and save you from yourselves."

I gulped. "But—"

As soon as the word left my mouth, I regretted it.

The chief turned to me, an *Are you kidding?* look on his face. "But?" he asked.

I swallowed again. "Daisy," I said finally. I gave the chief a pleading look. He had to understand. It was hard enough for the Hardys not to investigate; that was in our blood. But it was even harder not to investigate what had happened to someone I really cared about, and someone I feared more with each passing day could be in very grave danger.

To his credit, Chief Olaf's eyes regained a smidgen of their usual warmth. "I'm sorry, Joe," he said. "I know you boys care about her. But we're going to find her. You just have to trust us."

But I didn't trust him, I realized now, climbing into Dad's car to drive to school with Frank. I didn't trust anyone to find Daisy. Anyone but Frank and myself.

"So," Frank said as he pulled out of the driveway. (I was on indefinite retirement from driving, at my own request.)

"So," I echoed. I knew Frank had something to say. In fact, I was pretty sure I knew what he would say.

"We have to stop," he said quietly, turning off our street.

I was quiet for a few seconds. I knew what Frank was saying was true. But I hated it. I hated that we still didn't know what had happened to Daisy. I even hated Doug Spencer a little for not being guilty and letting us save her.

"I know," I said finally.

Frank glanced over at me. "I know it's hard, bro," he said. "But we can't help Daisy much if we're dead. We just have to help the police where we can. And we'll have to keep an eye on each other for the next few days. Whoever's sending the notes might not realize right away that we've stopped investigating. I don't want either one of us to get hurt. So let's stick together as much as we can, and watch each other's backs."

"Okay," I said. Sure. Fine. Whatever.

It turns out that life is incredibly boring when you're not investigating something. When your only goal in life is to make sure your brother knows where you are, and that you're okay. I'm a decent student, but I'd never paid 100 percent attention in any of my classes before, because in the back of my mind, I was always thinking over a case. Now I really tried to focus on things like geometry, and was shocked. Are people aware of how much of our studies focus on triangles? Triangles.

Before lunch, Frank collected me from our designated checking-in spot, my locker. I followed him through the crowded halls to the cafeteria. I had a horrible feeling that even my beloved lunchtime ritual—ordering the special, no matter what it was—would be stripped of excitement. Maybe the special had never been that exciting. Maybe it was just the thrill of sleuthing that made it seem that way.

"Come on, Joe," Frank said, pulling me out of line after he'd apparently paid for both our lunches. "You seem down. Maybe when we finish we could get some ice cream. Ice cream is fun."

But I could tell he didn't believe it. Sleuthing is as much

in Frank's blood as it is in mine, and I was sure he was feeling the same lack of je ne sais quoi—I did pay attention in French class—that I was. I wondered if this was how some guys felt about football. Computer games. Science fiction. Maybe everyone has their version of sleuthing to get them through life, or at least high school.

"Oof!" I suddenly ran into a huge, heavy object, and my tray crashed against my shirt, splattering Daily Special all over my henley. I'd rammed into Lamar Kendall, one of the biggest football players. A few spots of Daily Special clung to his football jersey too. He snarled down at me.

"Sorry," I said. "I didn't see you there. Hey, you must be really depressed now that football's over."

Lamar's eyes seemed to burn down at me. I could tell he didn't appreciate my sudden understanding of the meaning in his life.

Time for reinforcements. "Frank?" I said, looking around for my brother. "Hey, where'd you—?"

He was gone. How was that possible? Frank was so hot to keep us together. And now, as Lamar picked a pea off his jersey and smushed it into my shirt, I understood why.

"Frank!"

But before I could find my brother, a huge, burly arm reached out from behind and grabbed me. A gruff voice announced in my ear, "You're coming with me!"

THE RED ARROW

9

FRANK

I HAD STOPPED BY THE CONDIMENT STATION to get some mayo for my sandwich when I turned around and realized Joe was gone.

"Joe!" I called, looking all around me. He couldn't have gone far. "JOE!"

A gaggle of cheerleaders walked by, looking at me like I was crazy, but Joe was nowhere to be seen. I threw my tray down on the condiment station and ran back to the food line. "Joe? Joe!"

"Yes?" A smiling brunette turned from the line. Joanne Sikorsky. Darn my parents for giving Joe such a common name!

"Sorry—wrong Jo," I said, turning back the way I'd come. "Joe! Joe?"

But soon I'd made a lap of the cafeteria and found no trace of him. I even asked as many people as I could, but no one seemed to know where he'd gone.

Then I spotted it: an overturned and abandoned tray of Daily Special over by the nacho bar.

There's one person in the school who actually eats the Daily Special, and that person is my brother. Sometimes I think the cafeteria workers only bother making it to humor him.

I turned away from the tray with a sinking feeling.

My only job that day was to keep my brother safe, and I'd failed. There was a seriously screwed-up person after us. Who knew what kind of trouble Joe might have found?

My heart was starting to thump loudly. I could feel my breath quickening. I was panicking. Joe wasn't here, in the cafeteria—what if he'd gone back to our meeting place when we were separated? It seemed unlikely, but I had to at least check. Besides, it wasn't like I had any other ideas yet.

I ran to the doors and shoved one open.

That's when a bony arm reached out and grabbed my elbow. "Where do you think you're going?"

I turned around. It was George Flanagan, a small, freckly kid from my history class. He wore the bright orange vest of a hall monitor. Technically, we're not allowed to leave the cafeteria during lunch.

"Look, George, it's an emergency," I said, yanking on my arm, but George held tight.

"There are restrooms by the nacho bar," he said solemnly.

"Not that kind of emergency." I yanked harder on my arm and this time managed to throw him off. I slammed through the doors and ran down the hall, making for Joe's locker as fast as I could.

A shrill whistle sounded behind me, followed by George's voice. "Violator! Violator! We have a violation!"

Our high school used to have pretty lax rules, but things have gotten a little crazy since our old principal was convicted of extortion and several other crimes, and our new principal took over.

One big change is these hall monitors. You have to go through a special application process to become one, and in exchange you get a special recommendation for the college of your choice. The monitors are posted all over school, enforcing rules that no one cared about a couple of months ago.

Now as I skidded down the hallway, I saw two monitors emerging at a big intersection a few yards away. I whirled around to try another route, but George was right behind me—with another monitor.

I turned back around. The two I'd seen at the intersection were hurtling toward me. I had nowhere to go.

I slowly held up my hands. "I give—OOF!"

Before I could surrender, I was tackled from all sides, crushed under a wriggling pile of orange vests.

They took me to Principal Gerther.

Before they made him principal, he was just Coach

Gerther—study hall monitor, driver's ed teacher, and basketball coach.

As far as I could tell, Coach Gerther hated children, teaching, and happiness—qualities that made him an odd choice for principal. He'd also lost something like 80 percent of his hearing in Vietnam, so he yells constantly and doesn't understand why everyone else doesn't yell too.

"WHAT'S THE BIG IDEA, HARDY?" he bellowed now, pushing his fancy ergonomic chair back from Principal Gorse's old desk. "LEAVING THE CAFETERIA? DISRESPECTING THE MONITORS?" He gestured to a huge file on the side of his desk. It was easily the width of three dictionaries. The label on the tab read HARDY, FRANK. "I'VE BEEN WARNED ABOUT YOU AND YOUR BROTHER."

I cleared my throat, then yelled back, "I was worried about my brother! Am worried about him, sir!"

Gerther raised his bushy eyebrows. "YOUR BROTHER? ISN'T HE A CAPABLE YOUNG ADULT? WHY DOES HE NEED YOU TO LOOK AFTER HIM?"

I shrugged. It was a good question. "I guess . . ."

Gerther interrupted me. "I CAN'T HEAR YOU. WHAT DO YOU THINK YOU ARE, SOME KIND OF VIGILANTE? SOME KIND OF AVENGING ANGEL?"

Now he raised only one bushy eyebrow at me, giving him a sly look. He pushed the folder toward me, knocking his name plate in the process. It was big and gold, and read PRINCIPAL GERTHER in huge capital letters. It was much bigger than Principal Gorse's had been. Probably a gift from someone, I figured. Maybe there was a long-suffering Mrs. Gerther out there, her eardrums shot to heck, thrilled that her husband had finally made good with this huge and inexplicable promotion.

As I examined it, something caught my eye and made my heart skip a beat. It was just a tiny thing—nothing I would ever have noticed had Gerther not bumped the name plate toward me.

In the corner, in pencil, someone had doodled the symbol of the Red Arrow.

The huge, shady criminal organization we hoped we'd wiped out by catching Principal Gorse—but really, who knew?

My mind raced with questions as I looked at the huge, seemingly dense man before me.

Was it someone's idea of a joke?

Or was Principal Gerther working for the Red Arrow?

If I assumed Gerther *was* working for the Red Arrow, that led to all sorts of new questions. Questions like: Did this somehow relate to the monitors spreading all over the school?

And most troubling: Had Gerther done something to Joe, in retaliation for what we did to Principal Gorse?

Principal Gerther didn't seem like the sharpest tool in

the shed, which would make his involvement in a sophisticated criminal organization seem unlikely. Still, it would definitely explain why he'd been chosen as principal, against all logic or good sense.

But then . . .

"AAAAAAAUUUUUGGGGHHH!"

A female scream cut into my racing thoughts. It sounded like it was coming from the gym, just a few doors down. Joe! What if this scream was related to his disappearance? I leaped to my feet.

Gerther looked at me like I was insane. "WHAT ARE YOU DOING?" It took me a few seconds to realize that he hadn't heard the scream.

But I had to investigate. "I—um—I just need to use the bathroom. I'm sorry. I'll be right back."

I turned and ran out of the office and to the gym as fast as my legs would carry me.

Behind me, I could hear Principal Gerther yelling. "I CAN'T HEAR YOU. WHAT IS WITH YOU TEENAGERS? YOU ALWAYS INSIST ON WHISPERING!"

THE TRUTH COMES OUT 10

JOE

THE OWNER OF THE BURLY ARM DRAGGED me kicking and screaming out of the cafeteria. I was screaming, but nobody could hear me because the sizable bicep was shoved right up against my mouth. I hoped the hall monitors would stop us as he dragged me toward the swinging doors, but for some reason stupid George Flanagan just nodded at us as I was dragged past. What the heck? If whoever was dragging me into the hall had been unwrapping a piece of gum, boom: automatic detention. But apparently, kidnapping and assault: all good, see you in English class.

The world was really beginning to seem like a cold, cruel place.

My assailant dragged me down several hallways. I couldn't

see much past the arm, but I tried to keep track of where we were going by feel. I was pretty sure we were headed toward the gym. My heart pounded as I wondered what horrors awaited me there. Was this guy going to try to strangle me with a volleyball net? Suffocate me with a tumbling mat? Who was this guy, and why had he grabbed me?

He pushed me through a swinging door into a small, dank room. I could see fluorescent lights mounted to the ceiling, lockers on the walls. I could hear a shower.

Then, all at once, I hit the floor with an "Oof!" The sudden impact startled me and knocked the air from my lungs. I looked up into the face of my kidnapper.

Neal Bunyan?

"Neanderthal!" I cried, which is Neal's loving nickname. Neal is a big shot on the football team. Awhile back, Frank and I had busted him for using steroids. He was a rather vocal critic of ours until recently, when, as part of the whole Principal Gorse case, we worked with him to find out why the Red Arrow seemed to have marked him for punishment. Since then, I thought we were cool. I thought we were on our way to becoming buds.

Apparently not.

I struggled to sit up. Looking around, I realized we were in one of the locker rooms.

"You know, Neal, if you needed to talk to me, you could have just asked me if I had a moment," I said, giving him the crooked smile that I have been told is charming.

Neal didn't seem charmed. "I was asked to get you and bring you here," he said with a shrug, "not ask politely."

That's when I caught sight of something hanging out of an open locker. Something that made me feel deeply uncomfortable. It was a bra, and I realized all at once that we were in the girls' locker room.

I straightened up. "Neanderthal, I don't think we're supposed to be in here."

I tried to get to my feet, but Neal put a meaty paw on my shoulder and unceremoniously pushed me back down. "They're waiting here," he said.

"Who's waiting here?" I asked. What was going on? Was Neal trying to get some weird revenge on me by planting me in the girls' locker room? But why? Last I checked we were allies.

Neal looked at me morosely. "Do you want to know the truth about Daisy?" he asked in his deep, ponderous voice.

That made me sit still. "Of course I do."

Neal didn't say anything else. After a few seconds, I heard light footsteps coming from the shower room and turned to look.

Coming toward me were Jamie King and Penelope Chung.

I swallowed. Jamie and Penelope? I remembered Penelope's sharp words when we told her we were investigating Daisy's disappearance. Could they be the mysterious enemy who wanted Frank and me to stop looking into what happened to her? It seemed impossible. I couldn't imagine Penelope cutting a brake line, or Jamie wrangling a rattlesnake.

They walked over to the low bench Neal had dumped me next to and sat down. "Hello, Joe," Penelope said. Her cool expression gave nothing away.

"Hi," I said, waiting.

That's when I noticed that Jamie looked as uncomfortable as Penelope did cool. She was fidgeting, wringing her hands and looking all over the locker room. Finally she looked down at me. "Listen, Joe, we know you're looking into what happened to Daisy."

I nodded. "And?"

Penelope cleared her throat. "There's something you should know," she said, then sighed. "Daisy asked us never to tell you. We wanted to be loyal to her, but now—she's been gone awhile, and we're getting scared."

I raised my eyebrows. This was intriguing. "What is it?"

Jamie looked nervously at Penelope, then blurted eagerly, "Daisy had been flirting with this guy online! She met him in a college chat room about a month ago. He's a freshman at Redmond U. Two weeks ago, they started meeting up in real life."

I frowned. Totally not what I was expecting. "But two weeks ago, she was dating me."

Penelope and Jamie just looked at me.

Oh.

"She was seeing someone else at the same time?" I asked. The information hurt, but more than that, it surprised me. Daisy and I hadn't known each other long enough to make it into serious boyfriend-girlfriend territory, but while we dated, I thought she really liked me.

Was she just a really good actress?

Or maybe she really liked us both . . . ?

I was totally confused.

Jamie nodded. "See, that's why we didn't want to tell you," she said. Penelope shot a glare at her, and Jamie quickly added, "I mean, that and the fact that we promised Daisy we never would."

"I thought she liked me," I blurted. As soon as the words left my mouth, I heard how pathetic they sounded, but really, I was just trying to figure it all out.

Penelope looked at me with fake girl sympathy. In our investigations, I'd interviewed enough girls to know the difference between real sympathy and the exaggerated fake kind. "She did like you," she said. "She thought you were very cute, very nice. . . ."

She trailed off and looked at Jamie, who jumped in with, "But you were a little boring and kind of goody-goody."

Boring? Goody-goody? "But—but—" I stammered, thinking of all the adventures I'd had and how I was *so* the opposite of boring and goody-goody. On the other hand, why was I trying to defend myself? Was there something bad about being good?

Penelope gave me a pitying look.

"Chad was more dangerous," she went on. "He was a bad boy."

Penelope nodded. "He had a bad past. Drug arrests, hanging out with the wrong people. He told her all that was behind him, that she made him want to be good."

Jamie sighed. "But he could be mean to her," she added. "Even before she disappeared, Penelope and I were starting to worry. They would have these huge fights and he would call her up and just scream at her."

A chill crawled up my back. This did not sound good. Since Daisy and I had called it quits, I'd been worried about her taking up with Luke again, but now it seemed like something far more dangerous had been going on.

"Chad was really into the whole Death Ride thing too," Penelope said. "He kept pumping her for details. He thought it was really cool that he was hanging out with the girl whose dad owned the Death Ride park."

My heart thumped. "Why are you just telling me this now?" I asked, anger creeping into my voice. This was all falling into creepy, terrible place, like a jigsaw puzzle from the dark side. Penelope and Jamie looked at me sheepishly.

"Daisy disappeared a few days ago, on the G-Force. Now, out of nowhere, you're telling me that she was seeing this nasty guy with a criminal past who was super interested in the Death Ride?" I shook my head in disbelief.

Jamie looked a little nervous. "We think . . . we think he might have something to do with it," she said

I threw my hands in the air. "Ya *think*?" I asked sarcastically. I sighed. "Seriously, you two . . . I know you're not my biggest fan, Penelope, but she could be in danger. Frank and I could have been looking into this the night she disappeared!"

Jamie frowned, looking sheepish again, but Penelope glanced at her, then back at me, her expression still strong.

"When Daisy first disappeared," she said, "there was a little part of me that thought she had done it on purpose. There was so much going on, with Luke and Chad and the whole Piperato thing. . . . I thought maybe she just wanted some time to herself to think things over." She stopped and swallowed hard. When she spoke again, her voice had changed, become more raw. "But if she just needed time to think, she would have come home by now," she went on, her voice breaking. "She wouldn't want her dad to worry like this. She was mad at him for some stuff, but they were close. Now I think she really might be in trouble." She closed her eyes, and tears dribbled down her cheeks.

I slowly got to my feet, letting out a huge sigh.

"Thanks for telling me, I guess," I said after a moment. I still wasn't willing to forgive them for keeping this from me. This was important information. Information that might even mean the difference between life and death. It was clear to me that I was going to have to find Frank now, and we were going to leave school and go to Redmond and find this dude. "We'll try to find him."

Penelope nodded. She got up and walked over to the bank of lockers, where I now noticed a backpack was resting on the floor. She reached in and pulled out a sheaf of papers, then carried it over to me and held it out.

"These are e-mails from Chad," she said, swiping at her eyes. "Things Daisy forwarded to me. You can see how crazy he can be. But maybe the e-mails have something that would help you? Oh!"

A little chime sounded from inside Penelope's backpack. She ran over and pulled out her phone, glancing down at it.

Suddenly her face turned white, and she let out an eardrum-piercing scream.

I ran over to her and grabbed the phone. "Penelope, what is it?"

But when I looked at the screen, I understood.

LOOK N TEH LEMONADE STNNAD—MY LIEF DPENDS N IT!!!

The text was from "Daisy Rodriguez."

TOGETHER FOREVER
11

FRANK

I BURST INTO THE LOCKER ROOM JUST AS JOE was running out. We slammed into each other, but quickly straightened ourselves out. He was holding a phone in a pink rhinestone case and had a wild look in his eyes.

"To the car," he said simply. "We need to get to Funspot, pronto. We'll have to break in. Sorry, Hector!"

We ran down the hall toward the exit and pushed past the hall monitor—who was, thankfully, a small freshman girl who couldn't do much to physically restrain us—and out to the parking lot. We bolted to the car and jumped in. I backed up the car and was squealing out of the parking lot before the orange-vested army of monitors burst out the door to follow us. Their concerned, disappointed faces registered for a moment in the rearview mirror, and then we were out on the streets—free.

"Tell me what's going on," I said as I sped toward Funspot.

So Joe caught me up on what he'd learned. Basically, Daisy had been seeing a bad-news guy at the same time she was dating Joe. Penelope thought she might have staged her disappearance to get some time to think, which was why she didn't tell us right away. But now even Penelope was worried.

I have to admit that all this information gave me a sinking feeling. Scary, criminal boyfriend?

I wasn't feeling good about Daisy's chances, but then Joe told me about the text.

"The lemonade stand?" I repeated. It had to be the stand right near the G-Force. The stand where I'd gone to fetch lemonade when I was starting to feel like a third wheel on our first trip to ride the Death Ride.

Joe nodded. "Her life depends on it," he repeated darkly.

"That means she's still alive," I pointed out. It was cold comfort, maybe, but Joe and I knew enough about missing persons cases to know that this was good news.

"So does Chad fit the profile?" I asked, thinking out loud. "He really doesn't want to be caught—check. If his motivation was to get Daisy, of course he would want to do everything he could to keep us from finding him."

Joe was scanning a few printouts of what looked like e-mails, but he nodded and added, "Has access to Funspot—

check. If he has Daisy with him, she could get him all the access he wants."

I nodded. "He set up a fake e-mail account for Doug Spencer and hacked into the Piperatos' e-mail—check. If he's a college student hanging out in chat rooms, I'm guessing he has the ability and the means to figure out basic e-mail hacking."

Joe sighed, flipping through the papers. "But why would he have set up the Death Ride hoax?" he asked. "That's what's holding me up. If he just wanted to be with Daisy . . ." He stopped, frowning at one of the printouts. "Hmmm. Listen to this. 'I know you're fed up, sweetie, but don't worry. I have a plan for us to be together forever—no parents, no school, no frustration.'"

Joe looked over at me.

"That could fit a plan to abduct her," I said. "Maybe he knew she wouldn't go along with it, so he'd have to use force?"

Joe frowned, scanning further. "It looks like she was complaining to him about the Death Ride hoax—how scary it was, how worried she was about Kelly and Luke." He turned to the next page. "He told her not to worry about it. It would all work out for the best."

I raised an eyebrow. "Which would make sense, if he was behind the whole thing."

Joe sighed again. "Maybe he was trying to distract everyone so he'd have an easier time getting Daisy when he was ready?" he suggested. "Still, it seems strange. I was sitting right near Daisy when she disappeared. I didn't hear any kind of struggle."

I glanced at my brother. "Maybe she was in on it," I said quietly. "Maybe she wanted to run away with him, but somewhere along the way, it turned bad."

Joe didn't say anything for a while. When I turned to look at him again, he was staring out the window, frowning.

"Maybe," he agreed finally, in a small voice. "Clearly, I didn't know Daisy as well as I thought I did."

A few minutes later I pulled into the deserted Funspot parking lot. I pulled close to the fence, and we jumped out. Near the administration building, I knew, only a tall chain-link fence separated the parking lot from the park grounds. I figured my brother and I could scale it with no problem, and I was right.

Inside, Funspot was completely empty. The silence and the total lack of people were disconcerting. We were used to seeing Funspot full of life, laughter, screaming kids. But now it was so quiet, like a funeral home. Or a morgue.

I tried to push that thought from my head as we ran to the lemonade stand just across from the G-Force.

For the first time—maybe it was the lack of people and life, or maybe just seeing the park in the cold light of day—I noticed how run-down the rest of the park was, aside from the shiny, space-age shape of the G-Force. The stands and attractions all bore a fresh coat of paint, but many of them had roofs that leaned precipitously, or beaten-up interiors. It almost seemed like Hector had spent all his money on the G-Force, then had to scramble to make the rest of the park look presentable.

Suddenly a loud chime pierced the silence, making us both jump. We were only halfway to the lemonade stand. Joe pulled Penelope's phone out of his pocket and held it out to me.

There was a new text from Daisy Rodriguez.

WHERE R U?

COMING, he wrote back. "We have to hurry."

We turned a corner and suddenly there it was: the G-Force, the site of so many chills and so much heartbreak. After Daisy's disappearance, the ride's demolition had been put on hold. I felt a wiggle of fear in my stomach just looking at it. The front door hung open, and the ride almost looked as if it were leering at us. It stopped me in my tracks.

"There it is," Joe said, seeming to read my thoughts. He slowed to a stop beside me.

"The ride that Hector thought would be his salvation," I said.

"Which turned out to bring on his downfall," Joe added.

I took a deep breath. "Let's go," I said, reaching out to touch my brother's shoulder.

But before we could move, I felt something cold and hard pressed between my shoulder blades. I had been on the wrong side of an armed man enough times to know that it was the barrel of a shotgun, and my blood ran cold.

A creepy, raspy voice spoke up then: "You're too late."

CHAPTER 12

JOE

I TURNED AROUND TO LOOK INTO THE CRAZED eyes of Hector Rodriguez, who was holding a shotgun to my brother's back.

"Hector?" I asked, using my gentlest voice. "I thought you were in jail. Are you okay?"

It was a rhetorical question, really. Clearly Hector was not okay. He had wild hair and eyes, and he looked like he hadn't slept in days.

"Oh," he said now, the tension in his face disappearing, making his expression droop like a collapsed soufflé. "They let me out. Doug Spencer dropped the charges. He realized you can't punish a man who has nothing left." He looked from me to my brother. "Joe and Frank. I appreciate your coming to help, looking into the case, but it's too late."

"Too late?" Frank asked, turning now and rubbing the spot on his back where Hector had pressed the shotgun.

"I've lost everything," Hector went on, staring into the distance. "All my money. My daughter. Maybe my mind." He barked out a short laugh that held no mirth whatsoever. "All because of this stupid amusement park," he went on, gesturing all around us. "I wanted to create something amazing out of something seedy—to give kids the childhood I never got."

Suddenly Hector stopped, and his expression changed. His face seemed to crumple in on itself, and then all at once he was crying. "Instead I lost my own child," he said with a sob. "She didn't want me to buy it. I should have listened to her. Now I'm trying to sell it, but there are no buyers, and even if one came forward, I would lose money. No one wants to own the park where children have disappeared." He swiped at his eyes, the shotgun dangling in his other hand.

"Hector," Frank said gently. "Can you give me the gun? I know you don't want to hurt anybody."

Hector looked at him blankly. "The gun is all I have left."

Uh-oh. There is nothing—nothing—more dangerous than a man who thinks he has nothing left to lose.

"That's not true, Hector," Frank said in a rushed voice. "It isn't too late. We think Daisy is still alive. We just got a text from her phone!"

Hector's eyes brightened. "What?"

But before Frank could answer him, the phone chimed again. I looked down.

YOU MUST COME ALONE. MUST!!!! IF YOU WANT ME ALIVE.

"That's right," I said, shooting a look at Frank. "In fact, Daisy just texted me again, saying we should look in the administration building. Hector—can you unlock it?"

Hector's eyes brightened. "Of course!"

Before I could say another word, he spun and ran off in the direction of the administration building, not even checking to make sure we were behind him.

I grabbed my brother. "Come on!"

We ran toward the lemonade stand, our feet thundering on the blacktop path.

The lemonade stand had an open front where the lemonade was sold, but that was completely empty. There was a small door leading into a closed back area, but that was locked up tight. I leaned forward and tried to look inside.

"Where is she?" Frank gasped behind me.

I grabbed the phone and typed as fast as I could.

WHERE R U?

It was only seconds before the phone chimed with a response.

HELP

Then a few seconds later:

PLZ! HLEP M

My heart was pounding in my chest. I didn't know what to do. I didn't know what to do! Frantic, I texted back:

HOW? WHERE?

Seconds later the phone chimed again.

INSIDE

Inside where? My fingers twitched with the impulse to text. But before I typed anything, I looked the stand over again. That's when I noticed that the padlock on a chain that held the door shut wasn't locked—it was dangling. I lunged over, grabbed it, and unlinked it from the chain. Yanking the chain off completely, I slammed the door open and charged in.

It was less than a second before something huge and heavy struck me over the head. Pain exploded through my brain. I fell like a stone, keeping consciousness just long enough to see Frank pounded over the head and dragged in behind me.

Then everything went black.

13

UNMASKED

FRANK

ID YOU ENJOY YOUR SNOOZE?"

I came to with my head pounding. It felt like an entire fifty-story skyscraper had been dumped onto my head. I moaned, reaching up to rub it, only to find that every part of my body hurt now. Wait—where was I?

I blinked and looked around. I was in a dim room lit with small purple lights. Actually—I felt vaguely ill as I realized this place was all too familiar. It was the site of one too many unhappy moments in my recent life.

We were inside the G-Force.

"Boys? Are you ready to talk?"

That's when I noticed her. Standing over us, dressed in a sleek turtleneck sweater and jeans, looking like a million bucks. Not a hair out of place. Makeup perfect. An aluminum baseball bat sitting at her feet.

Daisy Rodriguez.

Seeing me watching her, she smiled. "Ah, Frank. I always suspected you were the quicker one of the two." She walked over next to me and suddenly kicked a huge heap that lay just a few feet away. The heap moaned, and I realized that it was Joe.

"Wake up, sleepyhead. I think we should talk about our relationship."

Joe moaned again. "You're so mean," he whimpered, which was both sort of pathetic and dead on, under the circumstances.

She smiled again. "I wouldn't have to be if the two of you would just take a hint," she said, sighing and running a hand over her perfectly smooth hairdo. "Really, guys? A rattlesnake? Cut brakes? Honestly, Joe, if I'd known you were this devoted to me, maybe I would have given you more of a shot."

I blinked, feeling a sudden clarity. "You're behind the whole thing. The hoax. Your own disappearance."

She laughed. "Oh, finally. That's right, Frank. And I suppose you want to know why?"

Joe struggled to sit up. "Your father's a wreck," he said. "He thinks he's lost everything."

Daisy's expression hardened. "Good," she said. "Let him see what it feels like for a while." She strolled over to the bank of cushy purple seats and sat down, letting out a sigh. "He gave away my entire future to buy this stupid park, this stupid ride. Before Funspot, I was set to go to Dalton Academy with Luke this year, and I had my sights set on Princeton! Now I'm stuck at Bayport with you losers, and I'll be lucky to afford community college. Thanks, Dad."

"But what are you trying to do?" I asked, attempting to hold myself up on my elbows. The room was spinning. "Okay, you punished him, good job. Why not come back now?"

Daisy pursed her lips. "I didn't mean for it to go this far," she admitted. "I thought the Death Ride hoax would be enough to convince my dad to sell the park. But it didn't work like I hoped it would, so I had to up the ante: disappearing myself."

She stood and walked toward Joe, looking down at him with a thoughtful sigh. "I actually did like you," she said. "Pity. When I found out you were some kind of amateur detective, I realized I had a problem. I thought I could control you if I hired you to look into Kelly's disappearance, but you two weren't as malleable as I thought. You actually investigated. Like, without me." She shook her head. "It became clear I'd have to ditch you. Although it is kind of funny—you're such a hot investigator, and you never noticed I'm kind of a computer genius?"

She smiled. "That's how I hacked into the Piperatos' e-mail and set up a fake account for Doug Spencer, to throw the police. It didn't work for long, but, well, it was an effective distraction. The cops haven't found me yet. But you two were getting a little too close. So I had to get Penelope to do me another favor."

Joe rubbed his head. "She's in on the whole thing," he said, seemingly just realizing it now.

Daisy nodded. "She's an excellent best friend," she said simply. "Very loyal."

"Wait a minute," I said. "Where have you been all this time?"

Daisy smirked. "Wasn't I just telling you what a good friend Penelope is? She also happens to have a spare attic bedroom in her house. I was quite comfortable there, and her parents never suspected a thing."

"But how did you manage to put Poky in our car?" asked Joe.

"I had Penelope's help there, too. She followed you to the prison after school and texted me where you were. Then she picked me up and we got Poky from the park, and it was a matter of moments to place her on the driver's seat." Daisy looked smug at her cleverness.

"What about cutting the brakes?" I put in.

"After Penelope told you about Doug Spencer giving me the side eye and acting suspicious, I knew you'd end up looking for him. So I snuck into your driveway Friday night and did a little job on the brakes, just to slow you down—or not, as the case may be." She chuckled. "Looks like they failed right on schedule."

I looked from Joe to Daisy. "Well, I'm glad we had this little talk," I said. "What now?"

She sighed. "Oh, Frank. Oh, Joe. I didn't want it to come to this, you know."

Joe looked unimpressed. "You mentioned," he said.

She looked at him almost sadly. "After you tracked down Doug Spencer, I knew it was just a matter of time until you figured out the truth. So you're going to have to go away for a while."

She walked into the center of the circle of seats and leaned over the railing, lifting up the carpet and running her fingers over the floor until she found the catch to the trapdoor that lay there. The door lifted straight up. My stomach dropped, and I looked at Joe, who seemed to be having the same horrifying realization that I was.

Zzzzzt! A blue spark shot out of Daisy's hand, and I turned to see that she was holding a Taser. "You're going to have to get in," she said, nodding at the tiny crawlspace where Kelly and Luke had hidden before being escorted to a hotel by Cal Nevins, the old G-Force ride operator.

Joe looked even more horrified. "Both of us?" he asked. "But—but—"

Daisy sighed impatiently. "It will be uncomfortable," she said, "but don't worry—I've put plenty of water down there, and a human being can survive up to two weeks without food! If it takes longer than that for my dad to sell Funspot, I'll come by and bring you some Luna bars."

"You're insane," I said, the truth dawning on me. The minute I realized what Daisy had done, I'd grasped that she was a little "off." But no, she was completely, utterly nuts. She was going to lock us in a crawlspace for two weeks? Until Funspot sold? Whenever that might be?

She narrowed her eyes at me. "I'm determined," she corrected. "And really, Frank—I tried my darnedest to warn you two. Is it my fault if you chose to put my well-being above your own?"

She pushed the buttons on the Taser again, and more sparks crackled at us.

"Get in," she ordered.

There didn't seem to be much point in arguing.

I looked at Joe, and we slowly got to our feet—my head spinning—and climbed over the railing.

"You first," Daisy said to Joe, and he gave me a grim frown before stepping into the crawlspace and getting down on all fours. The space was far too small for us to stand, and with two of us in there, we wouldn't be able to turn around or move much at all.

She turned to me and sparked the Taser again. "Now you."

I swallowed hard and stepped into the tiny space, struggling to arrange my arms and legs so that Joe and I could both fit.

Daisy grabbed the trapdoor. "Farewell, boys. Hope you don't suffocate down there." She chuckled lightly, and I was struck again by how completely crazy she was. Then she started closing the door. I swallowed and tried to steel myself against the claustrophobia, the horrible feeling of being trapped, but it was even worse than I could have imagined. The trapdoor came down and I almost stopped feeling human. We were just two animals, trapped down here, trying to stay alive.

At the last minute I moved my hand so that a finger covered the right side of the latch. I clicked my tongue on the roof of my mouth, mimicking the sound the door would make when it caught. I could feel Joe try to turn and look at me, but it was impossible in the small space.

We could hear Daisy sigh and then grab her baseball bat. A few seconds later, the door to the G-Force opened and we could hear birds, wind rustling through leaves—all the normal sounds of outdoor life. Then the door slammed behind her, and all was silent again.

When I was sure she was gone, I pushed the trapdoor open and stood.

14 TRAPPED

JOE

I CAN BARELY EXPRESS HOW RELIEVED I WAS when Frank opened the trapdoor and stood up.

"Oh my gosh," I breathed, grabbing the rim of the crawlspace and stretching my legs. "Frank, you're a genius."

He shook his head, looking around. "It was instinct," he said. "I didn't even think about it. I started to panic, and my hand just went over the latch." He sighed. "Anyway, we're still trapped in here."

"Or are we?" I asked. I reached into my pocket and pulled out Penelope's cell phone. Daisy had forgotten to take it back from me before she left us to rot away. I was still having trouble believing how completely cruel and messed up she'd turned out to be. But I didn't have time to think about it right now anyway—we had to get out!

I clicked the button to wake up the phone and squinted into the screen. No cell service; the thick walls of the G-Force must have blocked the signal. I felt the tiny hope that had lit up inside me snuffed out.

"No service," I told Frank.

He didn't reply, but just ran over to the side of the ride and started banging on it.

"HELLO! IS ANYONE OUT THERE? WE'RE TRAPPED!"

I came and joined him, banging so hard my knuckles hurt. "HECTOR! ARE YOU OUT THERE? HELP, PLEASE!!!"

We pounded the walls and screamed for what seemed like forever but, according to the clock on Penelope's phone, was only about fifteen minutes.

"The park's closed," I pointed out glumly.

Frank bit his lip, staring at the walls as if he could see through them. "Hector's still out there somewhere," he said. "At some point he has to come look for us, right? And he'll notice that the G-Force is closed when the door used to be open."

I frowned. I wanted to believe that, but Hector hadn't exactly seemed like himself when we'd last seen him. "I hope so," I said. "But he doesn't quite seem rational. And Daisy could be out there too, watching, ready to derail him if he comes close."

Frank walked back to the purple seats and collapsed onto

one with a sigh. "Think back," he said. "Who knows we came to Funspot?"

I shrugged, thinking it over. "Penelope and Jamie," I replied.

Frank groaned. "Penelope's working with Daisy," he said.

I nodded. "And Jamie's like her second best friend—even if she noticed something, I'm sure Penelope could just make up an explanation."

I walked over to the seats and sat down opposite Frank. "This is bad."

He leaned back, rubbing his eyes. "Nobody will realize we're missing till school ends, at the earliest. That's an hour from now."

I closed my eyes, thinking. Even when school was over . . . "Daisy's crazy," I said, stating the obvious. "And she has Penelope on her side. If someone noticed we were missing, she could probably distract them fairly quickly. Look how many times she distracted us from figuring out she was behind her own disappearance."

Frank grunted a response. We were both quiet for a few minutes, thinking our own separate thoughts. Then, suddenly, he jumped up.

"Hand me the phone," he said. I did, and he clicked it on. "See? It's a smartphone. Which means even if we don't have cell service, I should be able to turn on Wi-Fi."

He touched a few icons, dragged his finger across the screen, and then read, frowning.

"There's not much," he said. "Just a weak signal called 'funspot'—it must be the park's internal Wi-Fi." He touched something, then groaned. "It's password protected."

"Try the usual suspects," I suggested. As investigators, we'd hacked into a computer system now and again. It's amazing how often people use the same common passwords—things like "password" (as the Piperatos had) or "letmein."

Frank typed furiously, but I could tell by his little exasperated noises that nothing was working.

I closed my eyes and felt myself dip. Sleep felt all too close, like a warm blanket just ready to wrap itself around me. But by my calculations, it was barely one o'clock in the afternoon. I startled awake. "Frank—are you getting tired?"

Frank continued tapping away at the phone. "I could use a nap," he replied. "Why?"

I was starting to sweat, too. It was getting hot inside the G-Force. I looked around, trying to spot the ventilation system. "The ride isn't turned on, Frank. Are we going to run out of air?"

Frank didn't reply, but I could tell by the startled look he gave me that running out of air was a distinct possibility. He scratched his head and held the phone in his lap. "Nothing's working," he murmured.

I sat up, a thought occurring to me. It was getting harder to concentrate, and I didn't know whether that came from stress, lack of oxygen, or the fact that I'd recently been slammed in the head with a baseball bat. "Daisy is kind of a computer genius," I said. "That's what she just told us, right?"

Frank nodded. "Right."

I leaned forward. "So isn't it likely that she set up the funspot Wi-Fi for her dad?"

Frank's eyes widened. He looked down at the phone again. "Then she would have set the password." He held his finger over the touch-screen keyboard, then looked at me, waiting.

"Try Joe," I suggested. Recent events taken into consideration, it seemed like wishful thinking, but I still had to try it.

"No," Frank said.

"Hector," I suggested. Also unlikely, but who knew?

"No."

"What's her mother's name? Lucy."

Frank typed it in. "No."

I swallowed hard. "Luke," I suggested.

"No."

I sighed. "Chad," I said.

"No."

"He probably never existed," I said, realizing. "She probably made him up and had Penelope feed us the idea to get us over to Funspot. Man, I'm such a fool. Why do I always fall for the wrong—"

"Wait." Frank interrupted my self-pity party. "Daisy wanted to go to college, right? It was really important to her. What was . . . ?"

"Princeton," I said, remembering.

Frank's fingers danced over the tiny screen. His face lit up in a smile. "We're in," he said.

I jumped up and ran over to sit beside him as he opened up Penelope's e-mail and clicked the compose button. He addressed the e-mail to FunFunHector@Funspot.com and wrote,

HELP US! THIS IS FROM THE HARDYS. WE'RE TRAPPED IN THE G-FORCE!! WE FOUND DAISY!

Then he hit send.

We waited a few seconds. I half expected Hector to come charging in, but nothing happened.

"He may not be checking his e-mail," Frank pointed out.

"He may be sobbing onto his shotgun and flagellating himself, you mean," I muttered. Not to put too fine a point on it.

Frank opened the e-mail account again and quickly dashed off a few more messages—to Dad, to Mom, to Jamie King. It seemed like another half hour went by, and nothing happened.

I was beginning to lose hope. "What if the Wi-Fi signal isn't strong enough, and the messages aren't going through?" I asked.

But then I heard it. Footsteps charging up the metal steps to the G-Force, and a key turning in the side of the ride.

"Boys? Are you in there?"

The door swung open, and a bright shaft of sunlight shone in. A dark silhouette stepped into the ride and was gradually illuminated by the dim lighting.

"Hector!" Frank and I both yelled.

"You found Daisy?" Hector asked with a hopeful smile.

I nodded, shooting a sideways look at my brother. How to put this? "We, ah, have good news and bad news. . . ."

NEW BEGINNINGS 15

FRANK

"WOW," I BREATHED AS JOE AND I stepped through the familiar entrance gates to Funspot a few months later. "I'm getting major déjà vu—and not the good kind."

Dad stepped up behind us, clapping us both on the shoulders. "Come on, boys. I know this must bring back some strange memories, but we're here to support the community."

"That's right," Mom added, pushing her hair behind her ears as Aunt Trudy put on her beloved garden visor. "I, for one, am thrilled that Doug Spencer managed to get together the funds to buy this place back. I have lots of happy memories of bringing the two of you here when you were younger, and Doug Spencer was in charge."

Aunt Trudy smiled. "And I think it's lovely that those nice Piperato Brothers invested in the park, especially after they were falsely accused of staging those kidnappings." She stopped short of saying *by the two of you*, but Joe and I exchanged guilty looks, nonetheless. "It shows that they stand behind their work. I can't wait to try this new ride of theirs!"

It was true—Derek and Greg Piperato had made a major investment in Funspot, and so far, they really seemed to care about the park. The two of them had starred in a series of television commercials highlighting all the improvements they'd helped make to the park: "All-new food court! All-new games! And an all-new attitude: We want to make great memories for your family!"

Most notably, the Piperatos had designed an all-new ride, gratis, built where the old G-Force had stood. And tonight—at Funspot's reopening for the season—it looked like half the county had turned out to give it a try.

Honestly, the Piperatos, with their stripy zoot suits and waxed mustaches, made the perfect amusement park mascots. When they'd taken Joe and me out to dinner to thank us for helping clear their name—to the nicest restaurant either of us had ever set foot in—Greg told us that they were going to "scale back" their ride-designing business and just focus on Funspot for a while. "This has been, no pun intended, a roller-coaster ride for the two of us," he said. "It's helped us get our priorities straight. And I think it's helped us realize that what we really want to do is bring as much fun to kids' lives as we can."

The Piperatos weren't the only ones who'd rededicated themselves to improving kids' lives. When he sold Funspot—as he'd predicted, for notably less than he'd bought it—Hector had to "start over," as he put it. So he'd gone back to school to study to be a middle-school teacher. "I realize that what I really love is kids," he'd told Frank and me in a catch-up e-mail the week before. "This way I can make a real difference in their lives, before they end up like me or Cal."

"Hey there, Frank and Joe Hardy!" As we walked toward the line for the new ride, Derek Piperato suddenly leaped in front of us with a teeny-tiny video camera. "Have you come to try out the Glee-Force? You know what Greg and I are calling it? The Life Ride! HA!"

I smiled nervously at the camera. "Hi there, Derek. You're not getting back in the viral video business, are you?"

Derek chuckled and dropped the camera. "Gentlemen, certainly not. This is for our company website—no fancy editing, no effects. We're done with viral videos. We learned our lesson!"

We chatted for a few minutes, introducing our parents and Aunt Trudy, before saying our good-byes and heading over to the Glee-Force.

"Wow!" Joe exclaimed as we rounded a bend, coming up on the line. It snaked around in a few loops—definitely a healthy turnout, if not quite as crazy as the Death Ride days.

"There's Neal Bunyan and his sister Sharelle, George Flanagan, Jamie King," I said, pointing.

"Yeah, it's great," Joe said. "It looks like nearly the whole school came out."

I gulped, noting one of our classmates in particular. "There's Penelope," I said, pointing to the end of the line. "Oh man, we're going to end up right behind her. Awkward!"

We slowed, and soon my dad turned around. "What are you waiting for, boys? Let's get in line!"

We glanced at each other, then gritted our teeth and moved forward. As we got closer, we could make out the outline of the ride, a series of globular pink cars that seemed to twist around each other, float and dive in a dreamy motion. It looked really fun—sort of like the anti-G-Force!

"Hi, Penelope," I said as we stepped up behind her.

She turned and looked at us, clearly surprised—and not too pleased. But after a couple of seconds, her expression softened. "Hey, Frank and Joe," she said softly. "Listen, I'm glad to see you. I know I've been avoiding you lately—well, I've actually been really busy with my mandatory community service. But anyway: I really want to apologize."

I looked at Joe, surprised. "Really?" I asked.

She nodded. "I'm *really* sorry for what happened. So sorry. I was trying so hard to be a loyal friend to Daisy, I didn't even notice she was going off the deep end."

I nodded slowly. I could sort of understand what Penelope

was talking about. We all want to believe the best of our friends. And it's not like Joe or I noticed that Daisy was seriously losing it, until she tried to lock us into a crawlspace together for two weeks. After much debate and consultation with the authorities, it had been decided that Daisy would be sent to the Buchen Reformative School for Girls, a boarding/reform school in rural Pennsylvania. And actually, Joe had heard, she really seemed to be thriving there. She had a lot of friends and had taken up lacrosse.

Penelope sighed now. "And I'm responsible for putting you guys in a lot of danger," she said. "I feel . . . really terrible. There's nothing I can say to make up for that, except how sorry I am, and that I really didn't know."

I looked at Joe. Wow.

"You're forgiven, Penelope," he said. "We never held you responsible. I even forgive you for calling me boring and a goody-goody."

Penelope laughed. "She told me to say that!" she insisted. "It was all part of baiting you to go after her. Which—yeah. Seriously bad decision on my part."

Joe grinned. "So you don't think I'm boring?" he asked.

She grinned back. "Oh, I think you're boring as sin," she replied. "But I feel bad for letting you think Daisy thought that."

I was liking Penelope more and more. Time for a Cool Science Fact! "Hey, did you know it's scientifically possible to be bored to death?" I asked. "In London in the 1980s, psychologists interviewed a bunch of civil servants about how bored they were on a regular basis. People who claimed to be 'very bored' were four times more likely to die of a heart attack!"

Penelope looked at me blankly. *Oh no,* I thought. I'd been overconfident. This was the part where she would roll her eyes and look away, just as she had on our fateful blind date.

But then, to my surprise, she smiled and leaned in closer. "Actually," she whispered, "I read that study online, and I believe they were only two point five times more likely to die of a heart attack."

Then she touched my arm and smiled at me before turning back to move forward with the line.

I turned to Joe. "Did you see that?" I hissed, too low for our parents to hear. "She knew! My Cool Science Fact! She corrected me!"

Joe smiled and patted my shoulder. "I saw," he said. "I can't quite believe it, but I saw."

We all slowly snaked toward our chance to experience Funspot's newest attraction.

"Maybe Funspot will finally live up to its name," he added with a chuckle.

READ ON

FOR A SNEAK PEEK
OF THE NEXT MYSTERY IN THE
HARDY BOYS ADVENTURES:

PERIL AT GRANITE PEAK

FRANK

"HEADS UP, FRANK!" JOE SHOUTED. "Coming through!"

I glanced up from adjusting my boot buckle. My ski helmet made it hard to see. But my brother was impossible to miss in his red-and-blue jacket and tricked-out mirrored goggles. He bent low over his skis, poles tucked tightly under his arms and a big grin on his face.

"Learn to steer or you'll be back on the bunny slope, hotshot!" I yelled with a laugh as he whizzed past me.

Then I looked over my shoulder to check on our friend Chet Morton. Chet was the reason Joe and I were in Vermont, but that didn't mean he was an expert skier. Not even close. My eyes widened as Chet's skis almost crossed while he was negotiating an easy turn. He lurched and started to fall, but somehow righted himself.

"Nice save, buddy!" I called helpfully.

Chet turned his head and squinted at me. It looked like his goggles were crooked. He was picking up speed as he slid downhill.

Just ahead, Joe had executed a crisp stop and was looking back as well. "Look out, Chet!" he hollered. "Tree!"

Chet whipped his head around just in time to see the huge spruce hurtling at him. Well, technically he was hurtling at it. Whatever. The effect would be the same if the two collided.

"Turn! Turn!" Joe and I yelled at the same time.

Chet leaned hard to the left, missing the tree by inches. Whew! He lost his balance immediately after that, belly flopping into a large snowdrift.

"Close one," Joe called.

"Yeah." I frowned, tilting my head as I heard a weird rumble. "What was that?"

Then I saw my answer. The snowdrift Chet had hit was moving.

"Avalanche!" Joe shouted. "Get out of the way, bro!"

He pushed off, aiming straight down the slope. I did the same. Glancing back over my shoulder, I saw Chet scrambling to his feet on the uphill side of the moving mass of tumbling snow. Good. He was safe. Joe and me? Not so much.

There was a snow-covered pile of rocks just ahead, so I bent low, leaning into a tidy parallel turn to avoid it. I looked over, expecting Joe to follow. But he was still heading straight down.

"Look out!" I yelled.

Too late. Joe was headed straight for the rocks! And the avalanche was coming fast. If he wiped out, he'd be buried!

I held my breath as Joe reached the rock pile. He saw it a half second before he got there and bent a little lower, letting gravity take him up and over on its thin covering of snow. A second later he was airborne. One ski started to dip down, and for a second I was sure he was going to wipe out. But he recovered quickly, landing hard but squarely and then turning sharply to follow me out of the path of the avalanche.

Joe was breathing hard when he caught up to me at the base of the slope. "Nice skiing, brother," he said, lifting his fist.

I bumped it, then pushed back my goggles. "Nice jump," I said. "That was a little too close for comfort."

"Where's Chet?" Joe peered up the slope. The avalanche was over, and we saw Chet carefully snowplowing his way down the hill.

By the time he reached us, my hands had almost stopped shaking. "Are you guys okay?" Chet cried. "I didn't mean to do that!"

"Forget it," I told him. "We're fine. It's just lucky nobody else was on the trail when it happened."

Chet nodded. "Yeah. This place is even deader than Cody said it would be."

There were maybe three or four skiers visible on the

various hills within our view, plus half a dozen beginners on the bunny slope over near the lodge. Other than that, we had the mountain to ourselves.

Joe was already heading for the lift. "Let's try the White Rattlesnake Trail next. Cody was telling us about it at breakfast, remember? It sounds like fun."

I didn't answer for a second. The White Rattlesnake did sound like fun. Maybe a little too much fun for Chet. If he'd caused an avalanche on the relatively easy green circle trail we'd just negotiated, what would he do on a trickier slope?

But Chet wasn't saying anything, so I didn't either. Joe and I might be brothers, but that didn't mean we always saw things the same way. He was definitely the daredevil type. Me? I liked a little adrenaline rush as much as the next guy—as long as that next guy wasn't Joe. He already thought I was way too cautious. I didn't want to give him more ammunition. Besides, Chet was a big boy. If he didn't want to try the White Rattlesnake Trail, he could speak up and say so.

We were a dozen yards from the lift when we heard a bark. Glancing over, I saw a guy hurrying past, head down and hands shoved into the pockets of his well-worn parka. A large black-and-tan dog was at his side. Her ears were pricked toward us, and her furry tail was wagging.

"Cody!" Chet called, waving. "Yo, over here!"

Cody Gallagher was the one who'd invited us to Granite Peak Lodge. He'd been Chet's camp counselor years ago, and the two of them had kept in touch. Cody was a few years older than us, tall and wiry with reddish-brown hair. A little quiet, but a nice guy. He'd graduated from high school a year or two earlier and now worked full-time at the lodge with his parents. His trusty Lab-shepherd mix, Blizzard, never left his side.

Cody heard Chet and looked over. He was pretty far away, but for a split second it looked as if a shadow passed over his expression. Was I imagining things, or did he appear less than thrilled to see us?

But the moment passed quickly. "Hi, guys," Cody said, coming over. "Having fun?"

"A blast," Joe replied, leaning over to rub Blizzard's furry head.

I nodded. "But listen, there was a minor avalanche on the Sugar Maple Trail just now. . . ." I quickly filled him in on what had happened.

Cody listened, looking concerned. "I'll let my parents know," he said. "They might want to add that slope to the restricted list until we can check it out."

I nodded again. There was a notice hanging on the bulletin board in the lodge's dining room, listing several ski trails that were off-limits due to weather conditions or other issues. I'd had plenty of time to study it that morning while Joe and Chet were having a third helping of bacon and eggs.

"So where are you going?" Chet asked Cody as we neared the ski lift. "Hoping to get a few runs in?"

"Not exactly," Cody said. "Mom asked me to clear some branches off one of the trails."

There were only a few people waiting for the lifts. As we arrived, a young couple hopped into an empty car. Cody grabbed a well-worn pair of skis and poles that were leaning against the wall of the control booth.

"Guess we won't have to wait long for a lift," Joe joked as two more skiers stepped into another lift.

Cody grimaced. "Yeah."

I shot Joe a warning look. Leave it to my brother to bring up a sore subject. We all knew that Granite Peak Lodge was having trouble attracting enough visitors—that was the main reason we were there. A couple of bigger, flashier resorts had opened on the other side of the mountain recently, and people were flocking to them. According to Cody's dad, the skiing was better on this side of the mountain, but people liked the Wi-Fi and spa treatments and fancy gourmet food those other resorts offered.

That was why Cody had e-mailed Chet a few weeks ago, urging him to come for a stay over winter break and bring all his friends. He'd even sent a discount coupon for one of the lodge's nicest suites.

Chet had been all for it. Surprisingly, so had his parents. Or maybe not so surprisingly. They were going to a wedding out of state, and I guess they preferred to ship Chet out to the lodge rather than leave him home alone.

However, Joe and I were the only friends Chet could convince to tag along. I guess nobody else's parents liked the idea of a bunch of teen guys let loose at a ski resort.

That hadn't been a problem for us, though. Mom and Dad

had okayed the plan as soon as they heard about it. And I was pretty sure I knew why. See, Joe and I had this hobby—solving crimes. We'd been doing it since we were little kids. And we were good at it. We'd nabbed more than our share of bad guys, sometimes with the help of our dad, a retired police detective and private investigator. Dad didn't always approve of our tendency to put ourselves in danger, but he'd been mostly supportive of our sleuthing. He got it, you know?

But lately we'd run into some trouble. Legal trouble, mostly. Not to mention some bad feelings with the local police. Long story short, we'd had to promise to get out of the crime-solving business for good, or we'd end up in reform school.

After we'd helped bust a local crime organization known as the Red Arrow, though, Bayport's police chief (and our parents) relaxed the rules, telling us we could catch a few crooks now and then as long as we agreed to keep law enforcement in the loop. Still, we were trying to keep a low profile in the crime-solving department. Truth be told, I think our parents were hoping that getting us out of Bayport for a week or two might keep our minds off mysteries for a while.

And I figured they were right. What kind of trouble could we find up here?

Soon we were at the front of the line. The lifts only held two people apiece.

"Go ahead," I told Chet as an empty car swung toward us. "Joe and I will catch the next one."

My brother and I watched as Chet and Cody headed up

the mountain. A moment later we hopped onto the next lift, our skis swinging as the car rose into the crisp, cold winter air.

"This is awesome." Joe scanned the scenery. "I can't believe we've got this whole place to ourselves, pretty much."

"Yeah, you might want to stop mentioning that in front of Cody," I told him. "Especially after that weather forecast this morning."

Joe's face fell. "Oh yeah," he said. "Do you think we'll have to leave?"

I shrugged. The weather report was warning that a serious blizzard might be coming in the next forty-eight hours. For a while they'd thought it would skirt the area, but now it seemed to be aiming right at Granite Peak. Then again, there was still a slight chance it would all peter out. I supposed that was why my aunt Trudy called them "weather guessers."

"Not much we can do about the weather," I told Joe. "Let's just have fun and see what happens. We can make a decision tomorrow."

Chet and Cody were waiting when we arrived at the top. The lift dropped us off at the edge of a large, flat clearing near the top of the hill. Several trails started there, snaking off in different directions, with large wooden signs marking the start of each one. The signs included the trail's name, difficulty level, and a map showing its place on the mountain. A trio of twentysomething girls who'd been just ahead of us in the lift line were starting out down a black diamond trail, while a man dressed in a flashy red-and-white parka was standing nearby, adjusting his helmet and goggles.

"Great day for skiing, huh?" I said as I passed him.

The man turned and blinked at me through his goggles. He was in his early thirties, with pasty skin, thin brown hair poking out from under his helmet, and watery gray eyes. He turned away without bothering to respond.

Whatever. I shrugged and moved on.

"White Rattlesnake, here we come!" Joe exclaimed, using his poles to push himself along in the direction of the trailhead.

"Hang on, I think my buckle's loose." Chet knelt down and fiddled with one of his boots.

"Have fun, you guys," Cody said. "I'll catch you at dinner." He headed toward one of the trailheads with Blizzard at his heels.

While we waited for Chet, I watched the pasty-skinned man head across the clearing. He wasn't exactly an expert skier. He almost tripped over his poles, then got his skis crossed and almost went down. I was a little surprised he wasn't still taking lessons down on the bunny slope.

As he reached one of the signs, I glanced at it. Good. It was a green circle trail—the easiest level.

But my eyes widened when I took in the name on the sign: Whispering Pine Trail.

"Wait! No!" I yelled as the man pushed off and disappeared down the slope. I spun around and gestured to the others. "We have to stop him!"

CAN'T GET ENOUGH OF THE

Stay connected to Frank and Joe online!

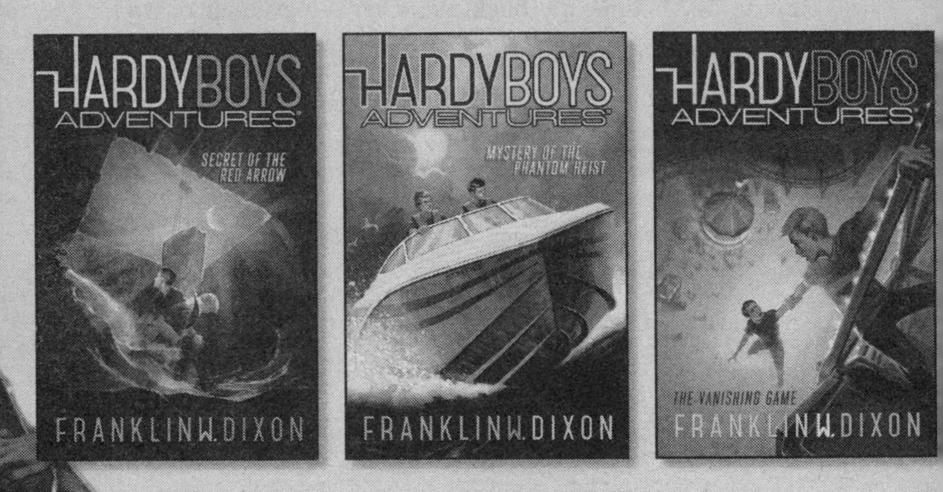

HardyBoysSeries.com

/HardyBoysSeries